Be sure to follow us!

Subscribe to:

Instagram@thegolfdiarie

FB@thegolfdiaries

Twitter@thegolfdiaries

YouTube@TheGolfDiariesGirl

Contact us at gwen@thegolfdiaries.com
for information on bulk purchases or
speaking engagements. The Golf Diaries
can bring the author to your live event.

Good

Smooches

Bunny

Love

Excited

Goofy

Not sure

Happy

Fun

The GOLF Diaries

Chloe's Choice

Gwen Elizabeth Foddrell

Throughout the book are underlined golf tips and terms.

Illustrations by Alphonzo Rodwell. Cover design by Gwen Foddrell. Creative collaboration Neil Branch.

For information on special discounts or bulk pricing contact www.thegolfdiaires.com or email at gwen@thegolfdiaries.com

ISBN-13 978-1505457292

ISBN-10 1505457297

This Diary belongs to

Chloe Castleberry

OW! OW! OW! OW!!!! Is this some kind of April Fools' joke? I thought for sure my pain would be gone by now, but my knee is killing me!

I'm Chloe Castleberry, and I am a figure skater.

And to make a long story short, I am taking 10 long weeks off from figure skating to rest my knee.

My knee is giving me sharp, shooting pains. When I try to do any of my jumps it feels like someone is stabbing me with a knife, just below my kneecap.

And sometimes, even when I am not skating, just out of the blue it will start hurting.

I went to the doctor and was diagnosed

with Osgood-Schlatter Disease.

When I first heard the name of what is wrong with my knee, I thought it sounded so weird!

I had never heard of it before, but come to find out it is quite common. Who knew?

Osgood-Schlatter?

Anyway, it is where the bone is growing faster than the tendons, and boy does IT REALLY HURT!

It has been 8 weeks since the pain became so unbearable that I could NOT skate.

But to be honest, I have kind of enjoyed the break from skating.

Sometimes I get tired of skating 6 days a week for hours a day.

While I am on a break from skating, my dad suggested I play golf.

He says my knee should be fine for swinging a golf club, so why not? I might like it. Maybe it will be fun? Who knows? I am up for anything!

April 2

My dad has played golf for the past 25 years, or something like that...anyway, he loves it.

My mom played too, but after she had me 12 years ago, well, she hasn't swung a club since.

She always says, "I don't have 5 hours for anything right now!"

She does always seem busy doing something.

When my dad plays golf with his friends he is gone about 5 hours, so I guess that is how long it takes to play golf.

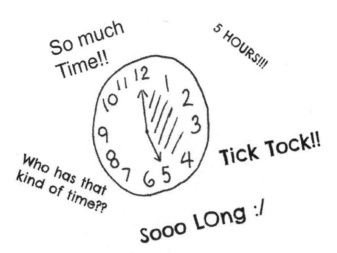

So much Time!!

5 HOURS!!!

Tick Tock!!

Who has that kind of time??

Sooo LOng :/

I wonder if that is how long it will take me to play?

Truthfully, if I am having fun, I don't care how long it takes.

I have a little brother, Caleb. He is 2 years younger than me. He is 10 and I am 12.

My parents are the "matching" type and like order in "their" world.

I guess our names both starting with a

"C" made them feel like they have order in the family.

We both have 5 letters in our names and our last name also starts with a C.

I must admit I do like the ring of my name "Chloe Castleberry," so I am not complaining. ☺

Most people think my brother and I are twins because we are the same height, even though he is 2 years younger!

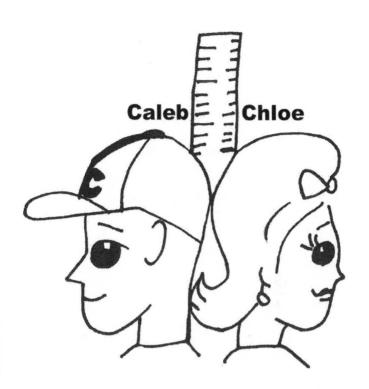

Caleb **Chloe**

Since we ARE so close in age and the same size, my mom does kind of treat us like twins.

She says it is easier if she can find activities where we can both participate at the same time.

For example, she put us both in learn to skate class at the local ice rink.

That is how I ended up being a figure skater, and Caleb an ice hockey player.

My guess is, if my dad is putting me in golf lessons, well, Caleb will be taking golf lessons, too.

Dad wasted no time signing Caleb AND ME up for 5 lessons at the local state golf course.

I guess he had been waiting for the day we said "yes" to playing golf! And Yep, I called it!

CALEB AND I BOTH!

I figured he would be joining me.

Honestly, I am kind of glad because we get along pretty well "most of the time." He is really good at telling people what to do and putting them in their place (if need be).

I, on the other hand, am NOT! I always try to be overly nice to everyone, and I don't ever want to hurt anyone's feelings.

Even if that means mine get hurt. ☹

Caleb isn't mean, but I guess being a hockey player, he isn't scared of confrontation or getting his teeth knocked out!

Actually, he would probably think it is cool to have teeth knocked out.

He would feel like it makes him look more like a hockey player. LOL!

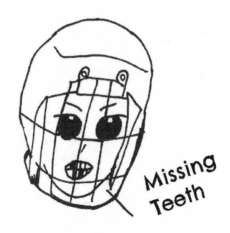

Missing Teeth

We went to our first golf lesson today and met our instructor.

I LOVED HER!!!!

She is into fingernail polish, loves the color pink, and all things girl.

Too cute!

Adorbs!

Glitter!

My brother, well, not so much.

He is not sure how he feels about a "CHICK" teaching him!

He makes the decision that he will be okay with it because:

1. Not that many people are around.

2. He doesn't know anyone here.

He decides to just roll with it.

There was another girl next to us on the range.

My coach introduced us. Her name was Tessa, and she is also 12 years old.

Our coach says she has been playing for 4 years.

She is actually pretty good. When she hits the ball it goes a long way and pretty straight.

I can't help but notice that her favorite color must be turquoise. She has a turquoise bag and turquoise clubs, and she is also wearing a turquoise hat.

I look down the driving range and see

another girl who is also hitting golf balls.

She looks about my age and is with her mom.

My coach said her name is Mackenzie. She is 12 years old as well, and she has been playing since she was 3 years old.

She looks like she is REALLY good! I am so excited to see girls my age playing golf here!

Maybe I can make some GFF's (Golf Friends Forever).

G ♥ F ♥ F

I would love to have some different choices other than the girls from the skating rink!

Overall, I had SO MUCH FUN TODAY!!!!!

My goal was to be able to actually hit the ball. LOL!

But I am totally shocked! I not only hit the ball, I even hit several good shots.

I couldn't believe it. It looks so easy hitting that little white ball, but it is harder than it looks.

The main point of our lesson today was our grip and stance. She really went over how important that is for a golfer.

At first it didn't feel right but I kept at it because I KNOW she knows what she is talking about.

I know using the grip she showed me is what helped me hit a few good shots.

I CAN NOT wait until my next lesson!

I am sure Caleb had fun too.

He always has a way with charming the women - it doesn't matter what age they are, they always think everything he does is sooooo cute, and our new golf coach is no exception!!

She was just oozing over him!

Everything he did she giggled and complimented him.

GAG ME!!!!

To be honest, Caleb did hit some really good shots today.

He was a little better than me. He is a natural at all sports, and it looks like golf will be no exception.

My mom said that playing hockey helps him with his golf swing because he has the whole eye-hand coordination thing down.

OH, and the BEST THING happened!!!!

At the end of our lesson our instructor invited both of us to play on the PGA Junior League golf team for the club. Not sure what that means yet, but it sounds exciting!

SQUEEEEE!!!!!!

I could barely hide my excitement!

I did tell our coach that I wasn't sure I would be good enough.

She insisted that we BOTH were!

She said it is a fun environment for kids to learn about golf rules and tournament play.

She said it is very laid back and low stress.

Honestly, that sounds like my kind of

sport!

She also said it would give us more practice time because the team has practice one night a week.

So, the team has golf practice once a week, and then we will have our regular lesson once a week.

I am SUPER excited!!

I never thought I would be playing on a GOLF TEAM, or that I would love being outside so much.

I mean I have never been one for bugs or nature.

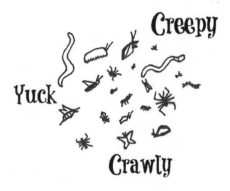

Creepy

Yuck

Crawly

Maybe it is because I have been in a cold ice rink for the last, you know, 5 YEARS!!

Being outside with the bugs really didn't seem to bother me at all!

I know it has only been one lesson, but I really loved being outside!

And wait...A tan!!!

I may actually get a tan for the first time!

I think I am going to love this golf thing!

Today I am having scary thoughts.

What if I end up liking golf better than skating?

What will I do???

I would have to break it to my mom that I like golf better, and my mom would be devastated!

I can see the tears now!

She is the one who started me skating when I was 8 years old!

She said she and her sister, Aunt Jana, always wanted to skate, but their parents didn't have the money.

She says she is giving me what they never had.

I appreciate it and all, but to me skating is just okay.

I go to the rink and I put in a lot of time- enough to be pretty good.

Some days I do enjoy it, but honestly I don't LOVE skating.

It is more like I LIKE skating.

I can't complain about my mom's efforts though, because my mom IS the best skater mom EVER!

She always makes sure I have the best costumes, best music, more lessons than most girls, and the best coaching.

I am just so worried because I know she loves it.

My aunt Jana loves it too.

She works for an airline, so she uses an airplane like most people use a car. Therefore, she has never missed any of my competitions.

The thought of telling my mom that I might not want to skate anymore makes my stomach feel SICK!!!!

Like I am going to THROW UP!!!

I know my mom loves to watch me skate, but I am just not sure I love skating.

Don't you think I would miss it if I loved it???

Oh well, I haven't made any decision yet, but honestly I can't get over how relaxing and how much fun golf is!

April 5

This morning, as I was lying in bed, I couldn't stop comparing golf and skating.

I know I don't know all there is to know about golf.

I have essentially only had one lesson.

My Dad did take us out on the course the other day to play 9 holes on a par 3 course, so from what I do know...this is what is going on in my head:

1. In golf you can make mistakes and as long as your next shot is good, you can cover up a mistake.

That NEVER happens in skating! You make one mistake and you are done!

Finished!!

Program OVER!!

Golf 1   Skating 0

2. When I went to the golf course, I loved listening to the birds chirping and seeing all the animals on the golf course.

My favorite animal to see on the coarse is a deer. My dad said it is not uncommon to see one or more deer running around.

The other day, when we were playing with my dad, a little baby deer was running back and forth and back and forth. It did it 6 times in a row.
I could not stop laughing! I just loved watching it!

In figure skating you are in a cold rink all day, and many times you are by yourself.

And let's face it...figure skating can be very lonely at times.

It would be cool if there were animals in a skating rink.

That would make it 10 times as much fun!!

Golf 2   Skating 0

3. When playing golf you can talk with your friends and have snacks while you are playing.

Also, if you are with an adult you sometimes get to ride in a GOLF CART!!!!

Riding in a golf cart is so much fun!

Skating - falling literally 300 times a day on hard ice trying to do a jump and getting bruises all over your legs and hips.

NOT FUN!!

Sometimes you even have mean girls pointing out just what you did wrong, or how they think they are better at it than you.

UM, no thank you! This is an easy point for golf!

Golf 3   Skating 0

---

4. In golf you must wear a collared shirt AND no blue jeans (at least that is the rule where we play).

However, you can throw your hair in a ponytail, or really any other way you want to wear it for a match, and go.

In skating you have to compete while looking pretty!

A lot of times that means skating with itchy costumes and wearing makeup that takes hours to do.

To be honest, it can be very stressful looking pretty while being athletic.

Golf 4   Skating 0

5. Golf is Objective! It doesn't matter who likes you, what you are wearing, or how long you have been playing.

If the ball goes in the hole in the least amount of strokes YOU WIN, and HARD WORK WILL PAY OFF!

Skating, not so much! Your hard work may not pay off.

A judge may not like your dress, your hair, your music, or just the way you look as a person and downgrade you.

It is not an objective sport AT ALL!!

Even when I watch the professionals on TV I get discouraged.

A few months ago I was watching the US Figure Skating Nationals, which is a competition that features the best girls in the USA.

One girl fell 2 times, and she beat a girl

who didn't fall at all.

And they had the same things in their programs.

The commentator on TV explained it and said the girl that didn't fall, didn't win because the judges didn't have enough confidence in her for her to win.

I just don't get it!

Golf 5   Skating 0

6. Golf is about learning life long skills. You can literally play until you DIE!!

There is one lady I saw the other day playing golf who is 85 years old. She was actually pretty good.

In skating your competitive career is typically over by the age of 22 to 23, and possibly before that due to injuries.

Mid Twenties is usually the age that most LPGA golfers are in the peak of their career.

Golf 6   Skating 0

7. One of the first things I noticed when we went to the golf course for the first time was how amazingly NICE everyone was to me.

Everyone I would speak to was always so positive and encouraging.

Several people said to me, "Work hard on your golf game, because there are lots of scholarships for girl golfers."

That is the total opposite from figure skating!

Every time you meet someone, the first thought they think...and sometimes say (which is RUDE) is "Oh she thinks she is going to the Olympics. She is going NOWHERE."

Such negativity!!!!!!

FINAL SCORE...

```
Golf 7      Skating 0
```

Okay, I HAVE to have a talk with my mom!

Hopefully she won't be upset, since she once played golf herself.

But, since I put this on paper, skating just doesn't make sense anymore.

Besides, golf is SO MUCH FUN!!!!

I finally found a sport where I can relax!!

Maybe that is why people play it all their life! ☺

April 6

Today I have to figure out how to tell my mom that I think I like golf better than skating.

It has been 9 weeks since I last skated, and I DO NOT MISS IT AT ALL! Don't you think I would miss it if I loved it?

But, you know what I would miss - if I had a DOG of my own, and I didn't play with it or see it for 9 weeks!!!

I mean, while I am telling my mom my true feelings why not tell her HOW BAD I REALLY WANT A DOG!

I can just see myself now with a cute little teacup dog named Talula.

I would carry her around in my purse.

I mean, I would do ANYTHING to have my

own dog!

My parents always say dogs are too much responsibility, but I AM RESPONSIBLE!

I have been trying to prove to them that I am responsible enough to have my own dog since I was 3.

One time I saved up my money and told my parents I would pay for it.

They said, "Dogs don't live with you, you live with them." I don't see the problem with that!

I have bargained with my parents every way I know how, and I have even recruited my aunt and uncle who have dogs to talk to my parents.

NOTHING WORKS!!!!

I always lie in bed at night and think of all the fun things I would do, and places I would go, with my dog in a purse over my shoulder.

I would get a cute pink zebra purse to carry her in and take her everywhere with me. I just know we would be best friends!

I love to watch the show *Dog Dynasty* on TV.

My favorite segment is where they teach dogs amazing tricks.

I would SO teach my little puppy cool tricks!

Especially the one where you make a circle with your arms and it jumps through your arms.

Good Doggie!!

My parents always say that indoor dogs make for a stinky, messy house.

They say they chew things, wee on the floor, and make stuff smell.

Since we live on a golf course, we don't have an option for an outdoor dog that runs around, so that is out.

I did see the most awesome article in the Golf Magazine that came to the house yesterday.

It was about this lady who takes her dog to the golf course with her.

She has a leash that hooks to her bag and her dog plays golf with her.

I think that would be AMAZING!

The article said if the dog gets in the sand trap, you must rake the sand trap after the dog.

Maybe while I am teaching my dog tricks I could teach it to rake the sand trap for me.

Maybe my parents would let me have a dog to go play golf with, especially if I could teach it to do cool tricks like rake the sand trap.

Hmmmm......I haven't tried that.

All I know is that one day when I get my own house I AM GETTING A DOG!

Anyway, I REALLY DO HAVE to figure out how to tell my mom how I feel about skating.

I know she already bought my dresses for next season, and my programs are already choreographed.

We did all that BEFORE I hurt my knee.

So I know she has already spent a ton of money on my programs for next season.

But, I have to figure out how to explain to her how I feel on the inside.

I could tell her all that money she spends

on my skating, she could spend on a
housekeeper to clean up after my dog! ☺

April 7

Okay! I have decided that for now I think I am going to say nothing.

I technically have another week before I am supposed to return to skating.

And, we have our first PGA Junior league practice coming up tomorrow.

I am so excited to meet more new people and see what a golf team practice is like.

Besides, I think that sometimes if you wait, problems take care of themselves, right????

Well, anyway, I am going with this philosophy for now, and maybe this problem will magically solve itself!!

Voila

Magically solved!

Anyway, I totally need to focus! I need to figure out my OOTD (outfit of the day) for my first golf team practice.

This is the REAL problem of the moment!!

I mean, I can't go there looking like a scrub!

I have to look AMAAAAAZING!!!!

I am just so excited because I never thought I would be playing on a real golf team!

I went through my closet, and I can only find one collared shirt. It is white.

I think I will wear that with a cute skirt.

I did find one cute skirt in my closet - it has built-in shorts, so it should be perfect!

It is of course PINK...my favorite color!

I just can't help but feel like this outfit I put together is missing something.

I think I need to add a little SPARKLE to it!

Maybe it is the figure skater in me, but this outfit needs some kind of BLING!

I whip out my nifty sequin stoner wand, some silver sparkly crystals, and get to work.

I am so happy with how this looks! I mean,
I must admit that this skirt looks
AMAZING!

Blingtastic!

OOTD!
Outfit of the Day

I don't know if anyone has thought of this or not. If not then I think golf may need to take a few lessons from the figure skating world when it comes to bling because this is PERFECT!

I am sure to draw some attention with this cute skirt! I can't wait until my practice tomorrow.

April 8

Ok, today was golf team practice and it went better than I ever thought it could!

It was so FUN!!!!

The club has about 45 kids on the team. So they made 3 teams with 15 kids on each team.

I was so excited because they put all the girls on one team together.

On our team we have 9 girls and 6 boys (one of which is my brother Caleb).

Most of the girls are 10, 11 or 12 years old.

With 9 girls on the team I should have some good options for some GFF's.

I was watching the college girls who had come out to play the course today.

There were 8 of them. They looked like they were such good friends.

They stopped by and said hello to all of us girls on the team. They were so nice!

One of the girls gave me a HI-5 for my outfit.

She said, "Girl, you are rocking that skirt!"

That totally made my day!!!

First of all she noticed and second she liked my skirt!!!

A college girl liked my self-designed, blinged-out golf skirt.

SQUEEEEEE!!!

When we got home from practice, my mom went onto the PGA Junior League website and got the rules for us to learn so we would know what to do tomorrow in our first match.

Some of the rules for the PGA Junior league say:

- You must be 13 or under to play.

- Both boys and girls hit from the same tee box.

- You play a scramble format.

- You play 2 people vs. 2 people.

- Competitions are team vs. team.

In a scramble format you and your partner both hit your tee shot. Then you choose whose ball is in a better position for a good 2nd shot, and then both players play from that spot.

You continue in this manner until you get the ball into the hole.

Other names for this type format are "Captain's Choice" or "Best Ball."

I really like the idea of not having to play my own ball right now, because even though I can hit some good shots, I can also hit some REALLY bad shots. It will be fun having a partner in case I mess up.

I am so excited for tomorrow because we have our first official PGA Junior league match!

We arrived at the course 45 minutes before our golf match.

We stretched, went to the driving range to hit some balls, and then practiced putting and chipping for a few minutes.

Before the match we walk into the clubhouse where there is a chalkboard that has everyone's name listed and who you are paired up with. Today the chalkboard looked like this:

Pairings for today		
Hole 1	Hole 2	Hole 3
Mackenzie	Chloe	Tessa
Julie	Ben	Rebecca
Isac	Charlie	Jennifer
Caleb	John	Hannah

For my first match I see that I got paired up with the BEST kid on our team.

His name is Ben. They usually pair a good kid with a new kid. So he is the good kid, and well, I am the new kid.

I am glad Ben is my partner because he will know the rules if I forget, AND we should have a good shot to choose from each time.

But that also means that we are going to play a top player from the other club's team.

We get to the first tee box, and YEP I guessed it. We are matched up against an 11 year-old boy, who is ranked number one in the state. He and his partner will be tough!

There is only one problem...I have not seen Ben yet. I am sure he will show up - maybe he is running late?

Having Ben as a partner, I seriously doubt we are going to use many of my shots.

My mom told me that when you play with someone really good, just try to focus on where you can help.

She said to try to focus on my putting.

I think it is going to be fun to watch how good my partner is and the boys we are playing against. I should learn a lot!

I am stretching and swinging my club waiting for Ben on the tee box.

Stretch

I have no idea where he is, I am trying not to panic, but time is running out!

Okay, I am starting to panic because I know I saw our names paired together on the board, but I haven't seen him.

I will FREAK if he doesn't show up!!!!

We only have 5 minutes before we tee off!

My heart is racing - I can literally feel it beating out of my chest.

This is the very first time I have EVER played in a match, and I CAN NOT do this by myself!!!!!

They call out our names, so it is our turn to go to the first tee box - it is time to tee off!

WHERE IS BEN???????? He is nowhere to be found!

Now is officially my time to go into a full-blown FREAK ATTACK!!!!

Just as I start to panic the coach of our team announces his name and tells him to report to the tee box.

HE IS A NO-SHOW! UGH!!!!!!!

Are they crazy? I CANNOT play against an 11 year-old boy ranked number one in the state by myself!

I am freaking out!!!

I know this is to learn and have fun, but I am going to get stomped, and that is NOT FUN!

And they will probably get frustrated waiting on me to hit AND find my ball!

With him being a no-show, thankfully, they moved a girl named Tessa to my team.

Hallelujah!!!!!! I am not on my own!!!

I am so relieved and glad, because she has been playing for a few years and in my opinion, is pretty good.

I already kind-of know her since we met on the driving range.

My coach introduced me to her and her dad.

She is the one with the cool turquoise clubs, and she seems really nice.

And because she is pretty good, I will try to relax and just have fun.

If nothing else, maybe I will make a GFF.

Golf Friends Forever!

Before we tee off we shake hands with the boys and introduce ourselves.

They then tell us that we can tee off first.

Tessa tells me I can go before her.

I really hope I hit a good shot on the first tee!

I don't know why it seems like such a big deal.

Maybe it is because there are quite a few people standing around, I don't know.

Anyway, I just pray I hit the ball straight

and get it off the ground.

I am thinking that I need to keep my eye on the ball and take away the club low and slow.

That is always what my dad tells me to focus on.

I start my swing and BAM!!! I hit the ball.

The course we are playing is a par 3 course.

A par is the number of shots it should take to get the ball in the hole. That means for each hole we have 3 shots to get the ball into the cup to make a par.

That also means we should hit the ball on the green with each of our tee shots.

Then we will have 2 strokes to putt it in the hole.

I didn't hit it on the green, but hey, I am happy that I DID HIT IT!

I will celebrate where I can! HaHa!

After Tessa and I hit our balls, they were both about the same distance.

Her ball had a better path to the green.

If we used my ball we would have to hit

over a sand trap.

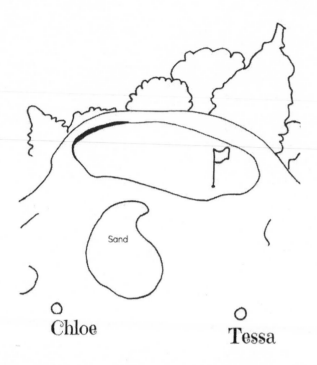

Chloe

Tessa

Sand

So we ended up choosing her ball.

I am just thrilled mine was even being considered.

It feels really good to hit a ball well!

My mom always says, "Nothing feels better than hitting the ball well, and nothing feels worse than hitting it poorly."

Since we didn't hit it on the green, we were chipping for our next shot.

I chipped first and I chipped it on the green. Yay!

I am just so happy I am not TOTALLY embarrassing myself!

We actually used my chip shot.

I am excited that I have contributed and we are not even off the first hole.

This may work pretty well if we can keep helping each other.

If we can one putt we could make a par. That would be AMAZING FOR US!

We putted, and neither one of us made it, but Tessa got closer to the hole than I did. I then knocked the ball into the cup for a score of 4.

WE MADE A BOGEY ON THE FIRST HOLE.
I WAS SO EXCITED!!!

I mean at least what we got has a name.

A bogey is when you get one over the par for the hole.

The boys we are playing made a par.

They, of course, hit the ball on the green with their first shot and 2 putted.

We didn't win the hole, but I am feeling pretty good right now.

If I were playing my own ball I may not have made a bogey, but with Tessa and I together, each getting a chance, we just might be okay!

On the next hole one of the boys sticks his ball right by the flagstick with his tee shot.

They are probably going to make a birdie.

 A birdie is when you hit the ball in the cup in one less stroke than the par.

I like the name BIRDIE.

I think it is such a cute name. I can't wait to get a birdie!

Tessa and I both hit our balls short of the green this time.

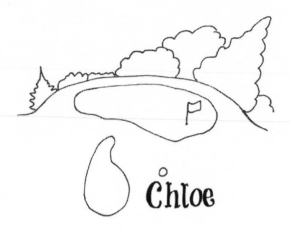

Chloe

Tessa

On this hole we ACTUALLY chose MY tee shot!

We may not win the match, or even win a hole, but I am having so much fun.

It is going better than I THOUGHT it was going to go, and I am not playing these boys BY MYSELF!

With our 2nd shot we chipped it on the green.

Tessa is really good at chipping! She put the ball right by the cup!

We then one putted, so that put us at par for that hole.

The boys made their birdie putt.

So, we lost the 2nd hole, which also means the boys captured the first flag.

In the 9 holes we play there are 3 flags to capture.

For every 3 holes you play, you capture a flag if you win at least 2 of the 3 holes.

Since they won the first two holes, they captured the first flag, which gave them

1 point.

The next hole has no pressure on it for us because there is no way we can win the flag.

Honestly, I am having so much fun, and I am so glad to be outside on this gorgeous day and not stuck in a cold ice rink!

And, I really like Tessa!

While we walk to our balls we have time to talk, and she told that me she has a passion for singing.

She said that one day she really wants to go to the Julliard Performing Arts School for singing.

When we were on the next tee box we had to wait for the group ahead of us.

You should never hit your ball when it could hit into the group in front of you. That can be dangerous and might seriously hurt someone.

While we are waiting I asked her, "What's your favorite song?"

She replies, " 'Shine Bright Like a Diamond,' because THAT is what I do."

Lacking confidence is obviously not a problem of hers!

She asked me, "Do you want me to sing some of the song?"

I raised my eyebrows, lifted my hands slightly, and said, "Sure, go ahead."

So she started singing, and actually, it wasn't half bad!

Shine bright

"Tessa, you did a great job!" I said and then I clapped for her.

The 2 boys we were playing against kind of gave a funny look to each other, but they clapped for her as well.

At that moment all I could think about was that people in golf are SO NICE!

I really don't care if we win or lose today because we are laughing AND SINGING. This is so much fun!

This match was not what I was expecting.

The only thing I have to compare it to is a figure skating competition.

And when I have a figure skating competition, I am under so much pressure!

I mean, I always feel like my head is going to pop off my shoulders from all the stress.

Stressed OUT!

Popping OFF!

And there is certainly no laughing going on when you are competing in figure skating.

I know they are both mostly individual sports, but golf is so much more social than skating, and I LOVE that part for sure!

I also enjoy having a partner and talking to the people we play against.

I mean, what girl doesn't enjoy talking and hanging out with friends for 2 1/2 hours?

In the end we didn't win the match, but we did tie the boys on 4 of the holes. Which I felt this was pretty good for US!

AND, we had fun hanging out, singing, and laughing.

We didn't capture ANY flags, but afterwards Tessa and I switched Instagram accounts and phone numbers so we can text and keep up with each other.

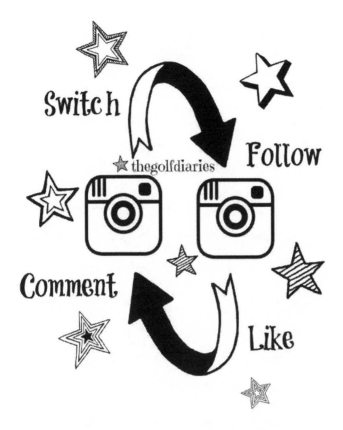

I got my first match under my belt and made my first GFF!

I think I am going to like this golf thing.

It is certainly a nice change!

Our house is on a golf course, but right now we don't belong to the club.

We used to be members, but my dad said when we were younger he didn't get to play much because babies are a lot of work.

He said if my brother, my mom, and I are all playing it only makes sense for us to join the club again.

So today we went over to visit the Palm Woods Country Club, also known as PWCC!

When I walked in everything and everyone was SO nice!

They even have a lounge where you can order food.

We sat down to order some food and talk with a lady about rejoining.

They brought us popcorn, chips, and fishy crackers to snack on! Who doesn't love FISHY CRACKERS!!!

Popcorn   Chips   YUM!!

Fishey Crackers!!!!

I could really get used to this kind of service! I don't know WHY we EVER left this amazing place!

While my parents were talking I happened to see the CUTEST boy walk in the door!

I mean, he can't be the cutest EVER, because that belongs to the one and only

RICKIE FOWLER!!!!!!

To me RICKIE FOWLER is SO ADORBS!

Every time I see him on TV, I stop what I am doing and just stare.

Then, when he makes a putt or bombs his drive I holler and chant his name.

Rickie, Rickie, Rickie!!!

It drives my dad CRAZYYYY!

But everything he does, I think, is AMAZING!!!!

I also follow him on Instagram.

I read in a magazine that he makes all his own posts on Instagram instead of having an agent do it for him.

That is so cool!!

I also read about how he has made some changes in his swing and is playing better golf.

Ok, I can easily get side tracked anytime I think of MY RICKIE!!!!!

BUT, for a real life boy, this one is definitely C-U-T-E!

He was wearing khaki shorts, a navy collared shirt, and a TaylorMade hat that was red. It seemed he had just finished playing golf.

He looks about my age, and as he looked over at our table, I was staring at him. OMG!!!!

I quickly looked away. I am so embarrassed!!

He **TOTALLY** caught me staring at him!

The director looked his way and said, "Hello Tyler," and she introduced him to the table.

She said, "Tyler, I want you to meet Chloe and Caleb. They are new junior golfers that are going to be joining our junior golf program."

Tyler replied, "Oh hey, nice to meet you. Hopefully I will see you around."

I cannot believe how many good things are

happening with this golf thing, but adding a dreamy boy to the mix just made telling my mom I am giving up figure skating to play golf a **NO Brainer!!**

C-U-T-E

April 11

Since we have rejoined the country club, my mom says we need a good baseline for where we are in our golf games. That way we can see our progress over time.

She wants Caleb and me to play in a tournament where we play our own ball.

She said it would be low stress with no expectations. Just to have fun! I am thinking, *sure, that sounds like fun.* ☺

A few minutes later I see mom getting off the computer and she informs us that she has entered us in a tournament where we have to play our own ball!!!

YIKES!!!

I AM A LITTLE FREAKED OUT NOW!!!

I didn't think she meant so soon. OMG!!!!!

This means no one can save me when I hit a bad shot.

And right now, being so new to golf, it is not IF, it is WHEN I hit a bad shot!

I guess the good news is we do have a FEW days before the tournament.

Mom says she has found a tournament where Caleb is the only 10 year-old boy, and I am the only 12 year-old girl.

That makes me a little less freaked out...I guess.

She said this is a small tournament on a par 3 course.

She said there are maybe 18 kids for all the age groups. So there is no pressure on us, and it is a great environment for us to learn.

In preparation for the tournament, my dad explained to us that **in golf you are almost always playing against the course, not against people**.

So even though we don't have anyone in our age group, he explained we should always try to do our personal best at playing the course.

I think that is why everyone is friendly and nice, because you are not against ANYONE but the golf course.

Even if it is against no one, it is always still fun to win.

In our state, each boy and girl who wins their age group gets a flag.

The flag is the kind that is on the flagstick on the greens. They have all different colors, and you pick the one you want.

Honestly, I am looking forward to getting one of those, and I can say I won my first tournament. Ha! Ha!

Even though I am against no one, every time I think about playing my OWN ball I freak out!!

But the pressure of this is nothing compared to the pressure of skating!

I mean, standing in a rink, all by yourself, with 5 judges staring at you, waiting for you to mess up, and a coach reminding you of all the things to think about, and to NOT MESS UP!

Yeah! I got this golf thing. I will be just fine!

One of my favorite things about golf is that if you make a mistake, or hit a bad shot, you just start over on the next hole. **No biggie!**

Yeah, That NEVER happens in skating! It is about being perfect all the time!

In addition to my last minute practicing, the other thing I must do to get ready for my first individual tournament is to do some SERIOUS shopping!!!!!

I mean, technically, I don't have any legit "golf clothes."

I am not looking for just any golf clothes!

I am on a mission to find some cute, blinged-out golf clothes!

Whether I am on the ice or on the green I am, and always will be, a blingonista!

I have been to a few golf stores and haven't seen anything to die for yet, so I think my best bet will be the Internet.

So I am off to the Internet for some SHOPPING!

April 12

Yesterday, while shopping online, I went to Google and put in "Cute girls golf bling," and several pictures came up.

There were some cute items that popped up, but no bling. ☹

If I am going to buy it, THERE MUST BE SOME KIND OF BLING ON IT!

To be honest, it appears to me that girl's golf needs a little help in this department!

I have been looking on the Internet for about 2 hours trying to find the cutest girl golf anything I can find, with bling.

I went to Pinterest and saw a picture of a girl wearing a cute skirt with ruffles. No bling, but it was cute!

I have scoured the Internet for this skirt and FINALLY found it. YAY!!!

Of course, the one skirt I find that I like is expensive.

My mom said she wants me to get it one size up so I can wear it longer.

She always does this with things that are expensive.

Fortunately, it has a pull cord at the waist, so it shouldn't be a big deal that it is one size too big.

The color I chose was-

Pink, Pink, Pink

of course!!!

Do any other colors really matter!!!

Mom says that she thinks I should get one in white and one in black.

She says that way they will go with everything.

I guess I see her point, but honestly, I AM A PINK GIRL!!!!!

She says if she is paying she gets to pick.

In a practical world, she is right. Black and white do go with everything.

But she doesn't think in practical terms when she is buying my skating costumes.

I need her to bring some of that "only the best will do for Chloe," to my golf shopping world!

Hmmm....maybe I will get them all ??

I am sure she is probably thinking this golf thing is only while my knee is hurt, and then I am going back to skating.

I decided to let her pick the skirt colors for me. I will then add my own touch of sparkle when they come.

I have been looking at golf videos on YouTube and honestly, it does seem like I see everyone wearing the color white in golf girls' wear. I think I actually will like having a white one. I guess I see her point.

But AGAIN, FOR THE RECORD...I AM A

Pink Girl!

After my mom ordered my skirts I did some more shopping on the Internet.

I need some cute tops to go with my skirts!

For my tops, I am trying to figure out

what size I would wear.

It is difficult because I am in-between a youth size x-large and a ladies size x-small.

I just don't know what to do, because my mom likes me to get at least a year out of my clothes.

She prefers 2 years, but she doesn't like things looking sloppy and big.

To figure out my shirt size, my mom took me to the local golf store, and I tried on different brands of tops.

I personally see myself in a PUMA shirt because it reminds me of - **RICKIE FOWLER!!!!!**

Every time I put on my Puma shirt, I will think of him.

I do love how happy and bold all the colors are as well.

I find a Puma ladies' golf shirt in size x-small, with just the right touch of PINK!

My mom lets me get this shirt, and I could NOT be happier.

This, with my skirt, will be the perfect OOTD for my first individual golf match.

♥ Twinning ♥

I did find one more shirt that was oh so cute, and of course, it was PUMA also!

In all, I picked out 2 Puma tops from the golf store.

I should be set now for my individual golf match and my next golf practice.

My mom doesn't know this yet, but I have plans to add a little bling to my clothes!

I will find just the right touch to make my outfits AMAAAZING!!!!

I am sure it is the figure skater in me, but who doesn't need a little bling in their swing? If there is one thing I learned from skating, it is how to stone and add bling to anything and everything!

Wardrobe ✔

So now, I need to start practicing on my game.

Bummer news! Last night my mom got an email that they moved the golf tournament she signed us up for to a different course and not the par-3 course she had picked.

It is now at a very popular semi-private course.

Semi-private means that you can get a membership to the course or pay by the round.

This course is much longer than the one my mom signed us up for. When the course changed, the tournament doubled in size.

It is pretty expensive to play the course they moved the tournament to and it is a big draw for junior players to get to play this course and only pay $17!

Normally it is $95 to play, so $17 is such a bargain!

They said we could get our money back if we weren't okay with the change, but my mom said that we already blocked off the weekend to play, so we might as well go.

So much for a quiet and small start to see where our golf games are!

It will still be fun, just a lot more difficult than she had planned for us.

One of the things about junior golf is you can usually sign up last minute, and it is not a huge deal.

AND....that is exactly what happened when they changed the tournament venue.

We went from playing on a small par 3 course to a long course in a big tournament.

It is not that big of a deal because we are playing for a learning experience, but it is a little intimidating playing such a long course.

I was looking forward to being the only girl in my age group for my first tournament.

12 year old girls

Before	After
Chloe	Sarah
	Chloe
	Judy
	Mackenzie
	Lori
	Jennifer

I know I am not good enough to do very well right now.

Especially, if the others who are playing in

my age group have been playing a long time.

It will still be fun because I do love hitting the ball, being outside, and walking and talking with the other kids.

So, for now I am going to focus on these things:

1. Looking cute in my new (blinged out) golf clothes!

2. Keeping my eye on the ball while hitting!

3. Trying to relax and have FUN!

In the junior tournaments, if you are 12 or 13 years old you _can_ choose to play in either the 9- or 18-hole matches.

My mom has opted for me to play in the 9-hole match. Since Caleb is 10, he automatically plays 9 holes.

For this tournament they have a rule that after you have **hit 3 shots over the par of the hole, which is a triple bogey**, you pick your ball up, take your triple bogey, and move to the next hole.

My goal for my first tournament is to NOT pick my ball up early, before I hit the ball in the cup.

April 14

OMG!!! My new golf skirts arrived in the mail today!

SQUEEE!!!!!!

My mom totally surprised me and got me the pink one too!

DOUBLE SQUEEEEE!!!!

I was only expecting the black and white ones. So when I saw the pink skirt, I totally flipped out!

I LOVE THEM ALL!!

They are so cute and comfortable. I know they are a size too big, but I don't think it makes that much difference.

I love them so much!!!!!

I think I should definitely be able to wear

these for the next 2 years. ☺

Now that I have looked at them and tried them on, there is only one thing I need to do...**ADD BLING, BLING, AND MORE BLING TO THEM!!!**

I am going to do the pink one first, of course!

I can't decide if I should use pink crystals or silver ones.

I put both pink and silver crystals on my skirt, and I think pink Swarovski crystals just can't be beat!

You can **NEVER** get enough Pink!

I think the silver ones will look good on the white and the black skirts.

So, **PINK** on **PINK** it is!

For the pattern I decided on a random placement.

OMG!!!! IT LOOKS SO GOOD!!!

I can't believe I haven't seen anyone do this yet!!!

For my hair, I really like being able to wear a high ponytail.

So, I think I will go with a visor.

I like both hats and visors, but I think I might like the visor just a little bit more.

I will put in my cute heart earrings with crystals on them, and VOILA!!

I will look like a BLINGONISTA!

I am so excited about my bling-wear, but in the back of my head, I am a little worried and can't stop thinking about my figure skating decision.

Today is the day I am supposed to go back to skating.

I am not going to say anything to my mom and see if she says anything to me.

Most of the time she is so busy, maybe she will forget. I can always act like I forgot also.

I know this isn't the best plan, but it is the only thing I know to do right now.

The thought of putting on skates and going back to the rink makes me feel like I am going back into a tense bull fighting arena and I just CAN NOT do it!!!

Here's to seeing how many days I can go without my mom bringing up skating!

Today is the DAY! Our first junior golf tournament where we play our own ball.

Funny thing is, I had no trouble sleeping!

I ate breakfast and felt totally normal all morning.

NO nerves!!

YUM!!!!!

Yogurt

♥BACON

This would never have been the case for me if I were going to a figure skating competition.

Not only can I not eat breakfast, I cannot eat at all the entire day I am skating!

And on those competition days, at the end of the day, I usually feel sick.

Sometimes I have skated my routine, and I don't even remember doing it!

So, for me to feel so normal is amazing!

Maybe it is because I know I don't have to **BE** and **LOOK** perfect!

I don't feel so alone playing golf. I do love how in golf you can choose to have a caddy with you. Usually it is a parent.

I hope I get my dad to walk with me today. He knows ALL the rules and what club I should use.

We arrive at the course and head to the driving range to start warming up.

I see Mackenzie, from my golf team, hitting balls on the driving range.

She is the girl my coach was telling me about that has been playing since she was 3.

I don't really know her very well, but let's just say I know OF her.

Her mom is standing behind her and seems very intense.

She kept talking and saying, "Good shot. You are really on today. You have a winning swing!"

Mackenzie is supposed to be pretty good! She is actually the same age as I am, so in my head I am thinking, *there's your winner of the 12 year old girl's group.*

I am walking to the mat to hit warm up balls. As I walk by, both Mackenzie and her mom stare at me.

I do see them checking out my skirt, and inside I am bursting with pride!

I am so excited, they noticed!!!

I mean HELLO...who wouldn't LOVE this skirt???

As I walk by, I smile, give a small wave, and say, "Hi."

The mom gives me a nod, and Mackenzie gives me a half smile and then goes back to what she is doing.

Mackenzie's mom proceeds to watch me out of the corner of her eye as I start hitting golf balls to warm up.

Thankfully, I am hitting the ball pretty well, for me. So hopefully I do not embarrass myself today.

My game plan for today is to try to make good contact with the ball each time. So far on the driving range, I might just be able to do that.

My mom tells me she is going to be my caddy today because my dad is going with Caleb.

I hear them announce the pairings for the match, and lucky me, I get Mackenzie (and her MOM who gave me funny looks) in my pairing.

Honestly, I am actually kind of glad, because I know you always learn from people that are better than you, so maybe I will learn something from playing with her today.

We walk to the first tee box. Everyone shakes hands and we introduce ourselves.

Chloe   Mackenzie   Julie

Turns out there will be 3 of us in the grouping.

Mackenzie, Julie (a 9 year old girl), and myself.

After we exchange pleasantries, Mackenzie's mom says, "You girls go ahead and hit. Mackenzie needs to wait until the group ahead gets out of her way."

It was kind of insulting for her to be talking down to us right away!

I shake it off and tee my ball up (but honestly inside I was still shaking my head at Mackenzie's mom).

I really hope I hit a good tee shot.

One way in which the skating world has helped me is that I have gotten pretty good at blocking out what others around me are saying and not letting it affect me.

I do the practice swings that my coach tells me to do before I hit the ball. I take my club back, swing through, and POW!

I hit a good shot!

I am so relieved and glad to start off with a good shot.

It makes me feel like I am not so out of place, since this is my first tournament.

I know it is only one shot, but I always get a little nervous on the first tee box... because of everyone standing around watching.

The other girl in our group, Julie, goes next and she hits a good shot, too.

Now it is Mackenzie's turn.

In my head I am thinking, *this better be good after her mother's comment.*

She steps up, puts her tee in the ground,

and places the ball on the tee.

She does 2 practice swings, stands behind her ball, walks back up to the ball, and readies to hit.

She takes the club back, comes through, and honestly, it was a good hit.

All 3 of us had good first shots on the first hole.

When we get up to our balls, we are all within 5 yards of each other.

Mackenzie
Julie ⊙   ⊙ Chloe

I am thrilled, but also kind of wondering why Mackenzie's mom thought she needed to go last.

Maybe that was her mom's way of letting us know that she knew her daughter was better than we are.

Who knows, and honestly who cares!!

My grandpa always says that, "If you are that good, you don't need to tell people-they will know!"

Her mom's comment was her way of telling us up front that her daughter is better.

I am sure we will know that she is better by the time the round is over!

We finished the first hole, and I did get a legitimate 3 over par.

I didn't have to pick up my ball, and I got to play the hole out, with a triple bogey.

Yay me!!

We walk to the next tee, and I was to tee off 3rd in our group.

The order for teeing off after the first hole is played, is for the person who scored lowest on the previous hole, to go first. This is called Honors.

For our group it was Mackenzie who had honors, of course.

When it was my turn to hit, I put the tee down, put the ball on the tee, and walked up to my ball.

As I start my backswing I hear Mackenzie's mom start yelling at me, "WHOA! WHOA! WHOA!" with her hands in the air.

It scared me to death!!!

I have no idea what is going on!! I am feeling a little panicked, and I step away from the ball, having no idea what I have done!

All I hear is her saying, "UM! UM! UM! Your ball is one inch in front of the tee blocks. YOU CANNOT HIT FROM THERE OR IT IS A PENALTY!!"

I pick the ball up, look back at my mom, and she says, "Honey, just move your ball back a bit."

The rule for teeing off is: the ball must be between the tee box markers or within 2 club lengths behind the tee box markers.

Ball Placement on Tee box

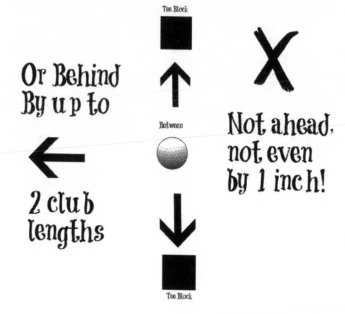

Tee Block

Between

Or Behind
By up to

← 2 club lengths

Not ahead,
not even
by 1 inch!

Tee Block

I had no idea!

First, I had never heard of this!

Second, I didn't do it on purpose!

So I moved my ball back "1 INCH" and hit the ball.

And there I learned my first new rule of

the day.

I'm glad I hit the ball okay after that display, because it is a little unnerving having someone holler at you while you are trying to swing the club!

We all completed the second hole, and I got another legit triple bogey. Yay!

I know that not everyone would be happy with a triple bogey, but my goal for the day is to **NOT** have to pick my ball up early on any of the holes.

I mean I have only been playing a few weeks, so I think it is a realistic goal, and well, so far so good.

A few more holes go by, and Mackenzie is teeing off first because she has honors again, of course.

As she is getting ready and starts her back swing, her mother starts screaming, "STOP, STOP, STOP," and runs up onto

the tee box and says, "Step away from
the ball!"

STOP! STOP! STOP!

Step away
from the
golf ball!

I was scared something awful had
happened.

I mean surely Mackenzie knows all the
rules, unlike me. I cannot imagine what
has gone wrong???

Her mom proceeds to tell her she is aiming
the wrong direction!!!

I am thinking, *ARE YOU KIDDING ME? I
CANNOT BELIEVE THIS!!!*

I would be a nervous wreck, if that were me. My mom would probably have to stop me on every shot, if I weren't aiming just right.

Her mom then realigns her, and now she has the green light to swing...I guess!

At this point I am scared for Mackenzie to hit a bad shot.

If her mom acts like that about being aimed the wrong way, I am scared to see what else could happen.

I mean, you know hitting a bad shot is coming, because every golfer is going to eventually hit a few bad shots in a round.

I find myself holding my breath every time she swings the club, because I can feel the tension radiating off her mom.

Honestly, crazy moms are NOT a new concept to me. They are ALL over the skating rinks!

But I feel bad for Mackenzie. It has to be stressful for her!

It happened, 2 holes later she hit a bad tee shot! Her mother huffs real loud and looks to the sky and slaps her hands on her thighs.

Unfortunately Mackenzie, who I am sure is now flustered, duffs her next shot too, and her mom is screaming at her through her teeth, in a low voice.

I am sure her mom thinks it is not that noticeable, but we can all hear her.

One thing I have noticed about golf courses is voices really travel loudly.

I don't know why, maybe the sound is bouncing off the trees...I have no idea.

HOW DID THEY HEAR THAT?

By now I feel so bad for Mackenzie, because no one is perfect. We could all hear what her mom was saying to her.

I know how tense it can be, when you are trying to be perfect. That is what figure skating is...a sport of perfection.

I know from first hand experience, perfection is very stressful!!

I start pulling for Mackenzie because I am scared of her mom having an outburst!

I mean, I really do like Mackenzie.

She seems very nice. She always says "good shot" when others hit a decent shot, and when the 3 of us girls all walk together in the fairway she is very talkative and nice.

Chloe   Makenzie   Julie

I am sure she likes walking with us, if for
nothing else, it is a way to get away from
her mom.

Honestly, I wouldn't blame her!

I tell her that she is a really good player
and I am glad we got paired together,
because I see her at the PGA Junior
league and it is fun to watch her play.

We discover we actually do have a lot in

common.

1. We both like horses.

2. We both have pink as our favorite color.

3. We both have a 1o year-old-brother that enjoys playing golf.

4. And we both like to watch *Dancing With The Stars* on TV.

This gives us lots to talk about. She said for my first time playing a tournament, she thought I was doing pretty well.

She also asked me where I got my skirt because she LOVES it.

I WAS READY TO SCREAM! I WAS SO HAPPY SHE LIKED MY SKIRT!

I love getting compliments on my BLINGTASTIC ideas!!!

I told her, "Thanks!"

She then asked me if I have an Instagram and I told her, "YES!"

She told me that she did too. We told each other our Instagram names so we can find and follow each other.

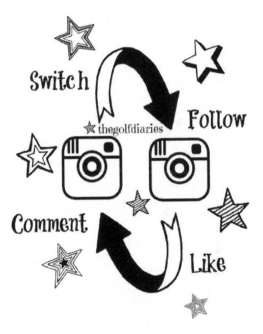

After all this, who knows, maybe we will be friends. That would be another GFF for me!

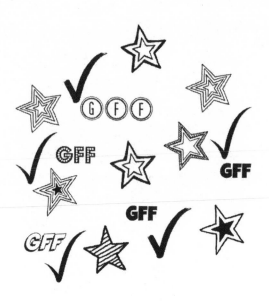

We finally made it to the 8th hole.

Good news!!! I have not had to pick up my ball early. Yay!!

I have even made one **bogey (which is just one over par).**

Bad news!!! I didn't know the 8th hole had water.

I hit my tee shot well...probably one of

my best shots of the day.

My second shot I totally smashed (for me). I am feeling pretty good.

But as we walk up to see where my second shot went, I see that it is just on the muddy edge of a creek.

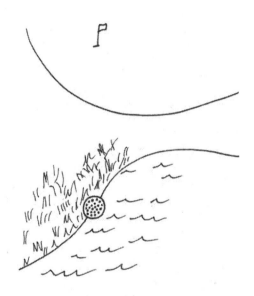

I ask my mom what to do since she is my caddy today and she says, "I guess try to hit it."

So I stand and try to hit the ball - I'm

not really sure what I'm doing at this point, so I take a swing at the ball.

It doesn't move much, but the little it did move made the position worse.

It went further in the creek! UGH!!!!

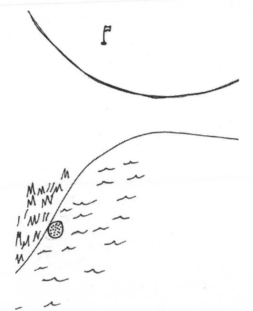

I guess now that Mackenzie's mom knows we are obviously not competition for her, she offers me some help and says, "Oh, there is a drop area right over here."

We had no idea about a "drop area," but

are thankful for the help out of this muddy situation.

She says they have played the course several times before, and you have to know the water is there because you can't see it on your second shot.

UMM....that information would have been helpful like 2 shots ago!!!!!

I guess the good news is, I learned something new....what a drop area is!

Certain courses will have an area marked off as a "drop area" for when you hit the ball into the water or a hazard.

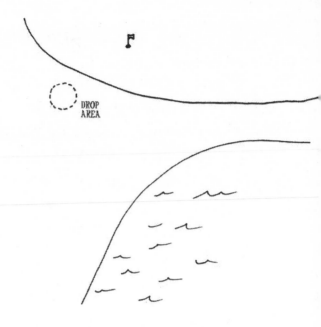

When you hit the ball into the hazard and use the drop area, you do have to add one stroke to your score, which is called a penalty stroke.

It helps me to think of it this way: one stroke is for hitting it in a hazard, and one stroke is for hitting it out of the hazard and to the drop spot. That helps me keep up with my score better.

In this case I had an extra stroke on top of the regular penalty because I took a swing at it while it was on the edge of the water. UGH!!!!!

I ended up with a triple bogey. It was a par 5 and I got an 8.

I didn't have to pick my ball up even with my penalty stroke.

So I am still meeting my goal of not picking the ball up, and we only have 1 hole left to play.

On to the 9th hole, and one hole away from meeting my goal.

I feel a little pressure to try and have something less than a triple bogey.

That probably sounds ridiculous to some people for me to say that, but golf is harder than it looks, and I am new and KEEPING IT REAL! LOL! ☺

So on the 9th hole - I ended up with a double bogey, which felt like SUCCESS!

My goal was to not have to pick my ball up early, and I achieved that.

I didn't win for my age group, but that's okay.

Mackenzie ended up winning for the 12 year old girls, but I did have a lot of fun.

12 year old girls division

Mackenzie

Even though I really wanted a flag! ☹

My brother got a flag for winning the 10 year-old boys division.

He actually had one other kid he played against, but Caleb had a better round so he won first for 10 year-old boys.

It came as no surprise to me because anything sports related seems to come easily for him!

He did, however, pick out a pink flag. He said it was for us to share.

I thought that was unusually nice of him.

So, all in all not a bad day!

I learned so much, made a GFF (who loved my skirt), and achieved my goal of NOT having to pick up my ball before finishing the hole! ☺

Now that we are members of the Palm Woods Country Club, we can drive over to the club in our golf cart, practice on the range, and do a little putting and chipping.

Today I was hitting balls on the range, and I look up and see Mackenzie walking over. She says, "Oh hey Chloe, are you a member here too?"

I answered, "Yes, my parents joined last week."

She replied, "Oh cool! Maybe we can hang

out sometime. You know, we only have to be 12 to play by ourselves. Maybe we can meet and play WITHOUT OUR MOMS!"

I replied, "I would love that!"

We exchanged phone numbers so we can text each other after talking to our moms about letting us meet up and play.

In the back of my mind, I can totally understand why Mackenzie would want to play without her mom!

I want to play without her mom and her

mom isn't putting the pressure on me.

Just as I am thinking that, Mackenzie's mom walks up. "Oh, hello Chloe. I didn't know you were members at Palm Woods."

I told her that we were, and that Mackenzie and I were just talking about how much fun it would be if we could play together.

Just then, my mom walked up and joins us and said, "Hello" to Mackenzie and her mom.

Her mom says to my mom, "The girls were just talking about how much fun it would be to get together and play. How about we get together as a 4-some?"

My mom replied that it sounded like fun, and they picked a date.

Mackenzie's mom said she would get the tee time and text it to my mom.

UGH!!! We wanted to play golf WITHOUT

the moms!!!

Mackenzie and I just looked at each other and shrugged our shoulders. I could tell we were both thinking the same thing.

WITHOUT THE MOMS!!

I couldn't wait to wear my blinged-out skirt to golf class today. I am oh so glad I blinged my skirt!

It just gives me the sparkle I need!

We were running a little behind, so I ran upstairs quickly to find a shirt for golf class, to go with my black skirt.

I couldn't find my collared shirt so, for class today I am wearing a shirt with some glitter on it.

It is not an "official" golf shirt, but it actually matches pretty well and looked cute with my blinged out skirt.

I am confused when it comes to golf shirts for girls having to "officially" have a collar.

I think if you look cute it will do, and people just want to see effort in your style.

The main reason I get so confused is because I love watching this show with my dad called *The Big Break* on the Golf Channel. It seems like many of the girls on the show don't wear a collared shirt.

So, off to golf class I went in my glittery "unofficial" golf shirt.

I really do like going to golf class. Today before golf class started, I got tons of compliments from the other girls on my skirt.

Everyone, of course, wanted to know where I got my sparkly skirt. When I told them I stoned it myself they couldn't believe it, and they all wanted to know if I could do one for them.

I told them, "Sure! Maybe they could come over sometime and we could have a

Swarovski skirt bling party." They all agreed they would LOVE to come over and do that.

So class was beginning and we all started hitting balls, and it didn't take me very long to figure out that the glitter on this shirt was a BAD idea and NOT going to work!

Every time I would swing, my arms would brush by the glitter on my shirt.

It felt like it was scrubbing the skin off my arms!

After about 10 swings my arms were RAW!

Thankfully, I had a light jacket in my bag.

Even though it was not cold I put the jacket on. Otherwise, there was no way I was going to make it through class!

My mom always makes sure I have a few essentials packed in my golf bag, at all times. The list looks something like this (after today the jacket is going to the top of the list):

Tees

Bug spray

Ball markers

Sunblock

Divot reapir tool

Light wind / rain jacket

Lip balm

Golf glove & backup glove

Golf towel

Golf balls

Tissues

Notebook

Water

Steel Brush for scrubbing clubs

Sunglasses

Pen / Pencil

Alignment sticks

A snack

I would really LOVE to add a Bushnell to the list of what is in my bag. They are so cool!

They look like binoculars, but they tell you how far away you are from the pin.

You just look in the eyepiece, line it up with the flag on the green, or any point you want to know the distance from, and push a button.

It then tells you how far away you are from that location.

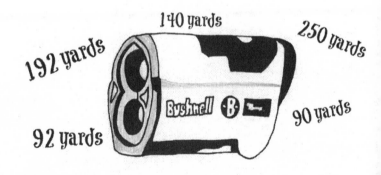

Knowing how far away you are helps you make sure you select the right club with more certainty.

I REALLY want one in my bag!!!!

I am hoping I get one for Christmas! Just saying!!!!

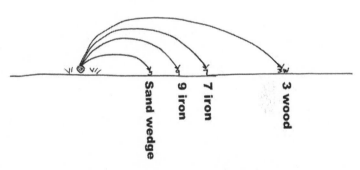 **The reason distance is so important is because you hit each club in your bag a different distance.**

My sand wedge is my shortest distance club. Then it goes 9-iron, 7-iron, and so on through my woods.

Once you know how far you hit each club, then you can select the right club for how far away you are from the green.

I have a junior set of clubs right now, so I

don't have all the irons the people on TV have.

But for TODAY, the most important item in my bag IS MY JACKET!

Because it TOTALLY saved my arms!

The most important item can change day to day. Like yesterday, the most important item in my bag was tissue!!!

My mom always packs tissues!

She says tissues are for blowing your nose. But also...for girls it can be useful if you NEED TO go to the restroom, and your only option is going in the woods!

Unfortunately I have had to use them for this on more than one occasion.

But, yesterday the occasion was actually for my brother!!!

I mean, boys have it good when it comes to going to the restroom on the golf course.

When they need to do #1, they can just go to the woods. No tissue needed!

However, if my brother is going to need tissue, it can only mean one thing....

#2!!!

And boy did my brother need the tissue bad!!!!!

It was about 6:30 p.m. and there was a nice breeze out.

The sky was dark, and it looked like it was going to start raining.

We had hit golf balls on the upper range and decided to move down to the smaller lower range, because we usually have it to ourselves late in the day.

It was my mom, brother, and myself who were hitting balls.

We decided to have a pitching contest from 40 yards away. We do this sometimes to make it fun to practice.

The object of our contest was to hit your ball onto the green and make it stay, without rolling off.

Whoever did it, got a point, but there was a sand trap in front of the green, so it was a little harder.

I had 3 points, my mom had 2, and my brother had 1. I was so excited to be in the lead.

Chloe	III
Mom	II
Caleb	I

All of a sudden my brother says, "MOM, I HAVE TO GO POOP!!!!!!!"

He starts running back to the golf cart.

My mom, seeing his urgency, quickly yells, "Do you think you can make it to the clubhouse, or do we need to go home?"

He yells, "NEITHER," and she then tells him, "HEAD TO THE WOODS!"

He runs to the woods, and almost simultaneously with running, he steps out of his shorts.

He barely made it before there was a massive explosion! It sounded like the air being let out of a huge balloon.

PHHHHHUUUUUHHHHHH!!!!!!!

It was spewing AND rifling out of him! My mom was looking around to make sure no one was coming.

I, on the other hand, was laughing so hard I physically fell over on the driving range.

My mom looked back at me, saw how hard I was laughing, and starting laughing herself.

My mom was laughing so hard I heard her say, "I am going to pee myself!"

Next thing I know she has pulled her pants down and is peeing right next to my brother.

If anyone came around the corner I would absolutely DIE!!

But I could barely breathe because I was laughing SO HARD!!!

SO, when I tell you it depends on the day as to what is the most important item in your bag - believe me! There was nothing more important than tissue to my brother (and mom) at this moment!

I was thinking today about the last time I was at golf class. I was listening to what some of the other girls were talking about, and I heard them saying that they were all doing something called the Drive, Chip and Putt.

One of the girls asked me if I was doing it. I told her that I didn't know what it was, so I wasn't sure.

When we got home, I asked my mom about it. She said she hasn't heard of it but will Google it.

My mom looks on Goggle for everything!

She says Google is like a magic 8 ball - she asks questions to it, and it gives her an answer.

What is <u>Drive, Chip & Putt</u>?

So I have no doubt she will figure out what the Drive, Chip and Putt is.

Well, my mom Googled the Drive, Chip and Putt, and it is a contest that the USGA (United States Golf Association) puts on for junior golfers.

It is free to enter, so of course my mom entered CALEB AND ME.

I still am not sure exactly what it is, so I went on YouTube and watched a few videos so I would know what to expect.

From the videos it looks like you hit 3

balls. Each drive gets scored by how far you hit it.

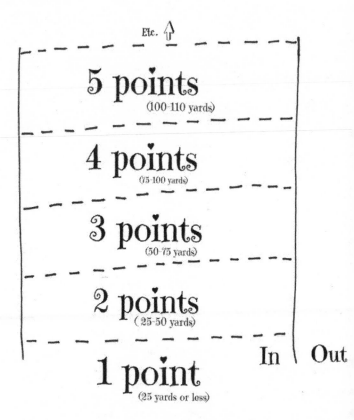

Etc. ⇪

5 points
(100-110 yards)

4 points
(75-100 yards)

3 points
(50-75 yards)

2 points
(25-50 yards)

1 point
(25 yards or less)

In \ Out

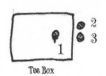

Tee Box

In order to get any points, you have to stay in between the two boundary markers. So you are scored on distance and accuracy.

Then you move over to chipping. You have 3 chips to a cup on the green. Around the cup they put 3 circles. The closer you hit it to the cup, the more points you get.

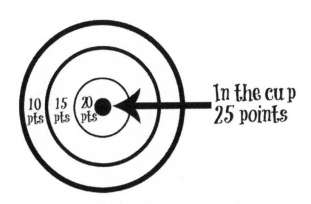

In the cup
25 points

Last was putting, and it is scored like the chipping. There are three circles around the hole, each with points in the circles.

The closer you get to the cup, the more points. If you get it in the hole it is extra points.

My mom said the contest is coming up in 3 days.

The contest is being held at the state course, which is where my PGA Junior League team plays.

I am excited, but I'm also slightly nervous. ☺

Now, when I say nervous it is a good, excited nervous - not a bad, feeling sick nervous.

I think the reason for the good nervous is because golf is a game of second and third chances.

Mistakes ARE going to happen, and it is OKAY.

I am not used to a sport where you can make mistakes. I find it very comforting.

When I was skating, I would get the kind of nervous where I would feel sick.

I think I felt sick because I felt I had to be perfect and I AM FAR FROM PERFECT!!!

I am excited that I get to participate in the Drive, Chip and Putt! Not sure how well I will do but I have yet to play golf without something good happening!

April 20

Today is EASTER!!!!!!!

I am so excited because I am hoping I get a dog today!!!!

I always hold out hope on holidays like Easter, Christmas, and my Birthday that I will finally get a dog!

So with it being Easter today, I am crossing my fingers that when I go downstairs I will finally get MY CUTE, ADORABLE, LITTLE TEACUP SHIH TZU DOG THAT I AM NAMING TALULA!

As soon as I wake up, I head down the stairs. I do see something furry, but it is so tiny.

I slowly walk up to the basket.

It is gray and fluffy, but it is not moving at all in my basket.

I didn't know if it was a stuffed animal or a real animal.

I reach down and feel of it – the fur is too soft for a dog.

I reach to pick it up and OMG...I got a baby EASTER BUNNY!!!!!!!!!!

Happy

Easter

It is not a dog, but it is an adorable little real animal I can put in a purse and carry around.

I am so excited I can hardly say anything.

I pick up my bunny and I see what else is in my basket.

I see some pink golf balls and candy, but nothing compares to my real live little BUNNY!!

I put my bunny back in the basket and took the cutest picture to upload to my Instagram account.

I have never had such an exciting Easter present!!

I love all animals, but especially tiny, fluffy, adorably cute, and soft animals.

SQUEEEEEEE!!!!!!!!

My new GFF's see my new bunny on Instagram and like my photo. Mackenzie comments: "OMG girl, what is its name?" I think for a minute and I write, "I have no idea, comment for any name ideas."

Different people chime in with, "Fluffy, Hop-Hop, Cottontail," but Mackenzie says, "How about Putt!"

I think about it for a minute, and I actually really like it.

I comment back,"Thanks Kinz! Putt, I love it!"

Mackenzie comments, "Hahahaha, no problem!!!"

So I tell my family I have named my bunny "Putt." Thankfully my family loves the name too.

I just CAN'T put my bunny down!!!!

Awwww Putt

I carry him around with me all day! If he could sleep with me in my room, I would keep him with me 24/7!

......ZZZZZ

But even Putt hasn't made me forget that
I still have to talk to my mom about not
going back to skating.

I can't believe she hasn't said anything to
me yet. I wonder if she is waiting for me
to go to her?

Either way, I am sticking with
procrastination for now!

As I have some skating thoughts on my mind, I start thinking about all the pressure you have on you when you have been participating in a sport for a long time, versus being new to a sport.

When you are new to a sport you have no expectations on your success. Really any success is a pleasant surprise and celebrated!

And, when you have a bad or disappointing performance it is no big deal because you're new, and there are little to no expectations.

But the opposite is true when you have been playing a sport for 4 or 5 years.

You are expected to perform, and when you don't perform, it can be such a disappointing feeling.

I think it all has to do with your expectations.

My Grandpa is a counselor, and he has always told me that unmet expectations are a major source of disappointment and anger.

I know that there are no expectations for me right now in golf, which is probably why it is all so fun, but every time I play golf, it is a predictably good and relaxing time.

April 22

OKAY...today is the day of the Drive, Chip and Putt contest!!!!

I know there are no expectations for me, but I am so excited!!!

Even though I have watched videos on YouTube, I still am not exactly sure what to expect.

When we pull up to the course, there is a tent set up outside.

When you sign in, they give you a goody bag with a towel, balls, and some knick-knack stuff. IT'S PRETTY NEAT!!!

Drive,
Chip
& Putt

My brother and I signed in, collected the goodies, and then headed to the range to warm up.

I must admit that my stomach is a little fluttery with nerves.

Feels like these are in my stomach

I think it is because I haven't been playing very long, and I hope I don't come in last place.

I hope I don't come in last!

Worried!

There were lots of kids practicing for the competition, and they had a big board up with everyone's name on it.

There are several girls listed on the board, who are on my PGA Junior League team.

Almost all of them have been playing much longer than me.

Again, I hope I don't come in last!

They gathered everyone and said it was time to start.

First was the driving part of the competition.

They divided us by gender and age. The youngest age went first.

Since Caleb is younger than I am, he went before me.

It was kind of nice because I could see how it worked before it was my turn.

The object of the drive was to see how far you could hit the ball, while keeping it in between the yellow stakes they placed out on the range.

So far, it was just like the video I saw on YouTube, and that helped me relax a tiny bit.

They give you three balls to hit, and your ball must land in between the stakes to receive any points.

You get points for how far you hit the ball, but your points ONLY count if it is in bounds.

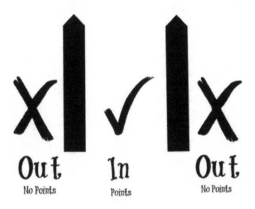

Out
No Points

In
Points

Out
No Points

Then they total up the points from all 3 of your shots.

I was so happy for my brother Caleb - he actually did pretty well!

There is one boy, Ben, who is amazing!

He is the boy I was paired with that didn't show up at the PGA Junior League match.

My brother came in 2nd place to Ben in the driving.

I was so happy for him!

I couldn't believe he beat so many other kids.

He was in the boys' 10-11 year old age group.

He just turned 10, and some of the 11 year olds were so much bigger than him!

It just goes to show that you can never tell by looking at a person in golf just who is good and who is not.

It reminds me of the saying, "Don't judge a book by its cover."

Caleb came in 2nd place in driving but finished 4th place overall.

I was so proud of him. I thought that was really good for him.

Only the top 3 for the age group advance to regionals.

He did receive a ribbon for his second place finish in the driving contest, which was really cool.

Yay!

2nd

Ok, now that my brother has gone, the next group up is mine.

Up first was my new GFF, Tessa.

She chose to bring her own brand new turquoise golf balls to hit.

I had never seen such cool golf balls before!

I can't believe she is going to waste them!

I guess it was to make a statement, but it seemed like a waste of money to me, since they were supplying balls for us, for free! She won't get the turquoise ones back!

She hit all her balls way left (which is called hooking the ball) and out of bounds, so she didn't get any points for the driving part.

I guess she thought she would hit the turquoise balls better, but the color of the ball doesn't make you hit the ball any better or any farther.

She actually is a good golfer, but in golf, just like in life, you always have good and bad days.

Maybe she is having a bad day. ☹

Next up is Mackenzie.

She also brought her own golf balls and hers are neon pink.

I ♥ Pink!!!

I am starting to wonder if all the girls my age brought their own golf balls, and am I going to be the only one who uses the range balls that are provided for free?

Mackenzie is a REALLY good golfer, and she hit her first ball really well.

She whispered to me that she is so

nervous that her knees are shaking.

There was a pretty big audience at the event, but for me, this was nothing.

I find it way more stressful to be the only person standing in the middle of an ice rink with 5 pair of eyes staring at you just waiting to judge you, and looking for any flaws!

I think this will be a piece of cake compared to that!

I told Mackenzie to relax, that she is a good golfer.

She hit her next shot and it went out of bounds.

She has one shot left to try to score some points.

She hit it, and it went pretty far and straight.

I was still thinking, *I CAN'T believe they threw away those cool, cute golf balls,* when they called my name.

I mean, seriously, who throws away golf balls like that!

Especially when they are neon pink golf balls.

I ♥ Pink!!!

I would love to have had those golf balls in my bag, and she wasted them on a DRIVING RANGE!

How stupid! I of course didn't say that, but I was thinking that in my head.

All right! I need to focus!! It is my turn.

I was a bit nervous, but not as much as I thought I would be.

Maybe it is because I am new, and you know, the whole no expectations thing.

But, I DON'T want to come in last! I really want to try to hit the ball well!

I pick up the FREE golf balls they gave me (and it didn't cost me or my parents a dime).

I place my first ball on the tee, stand

over the ball, and take my best swing.

I HIT THE BALL, IT WENT STRAIGHT, AND I SCORED SOME POINTS!

WOOHOO!!!

I was so excited!!

I know I still have 2 more to go, but I was off to a good start.

The next 2 balls I hit were about the same as my first one.

So for me, I did pretty well! I couldn't believe it!

I was so happy I wasn't going to be in last place!

Not being very nervous in front of crowds, might be one place where my figure skating has helped me.

In skating you have to be very mentally tough and I can't help but think that will help me in golf.

They gathered us together and announced the results. For the driver part of the competition I took 2nd!!!

Not only did I not get LAST place...I got 2nd place and a ribbon!!!

I was feeling so good! Mackenzie, of course, took first.

Next was the chipping part of the competition.

I was thinking I had this in the bag, because I thought chipping was the best part of my game.

But, I didn't do as well as I thought I

would.

The object of this part was to get the ball as close as you can to the hole or, even better, in the hole.

Unfortunately, ALL of mine were out of bounds. ☹

It was only out by an inch, which stunk because I did not hit them badly.

I actually did hit them inside the circles, but they rolled out, so I hit it just a little too hard. ☹

So on to the putting I go to finish up.

Putting is fun, but it takes some concentration.

I did pretty well for me but not good enough to place.

I took 4th place overall.

This isn't bad considering the fact that this was MY FIRST TIME EVER!

And I have only been playing for a few weeks!

There have been skating competitions where I didn't place as high as 4th after skating for years, so I am pretty happy with it!

It was a fun day, but more importantly, I know what I need to practice on for next year.

I was lying in bed last night thinking about the Drive, Chip and Putt.

I was thinking about how if a new girl went to the skating rink and had just started skating, there is no way she would

EVER be able to compete with girls who have been doing it for years, and she certainly would not place in the event.

It is really encouraging that there are no judges opinions as to who they feel is deserving in golf.

You make your own results and that is what it boils down to - YOUR results.

In golf it doesn't matter how long you have been playing, how you look, what you are wearing, if anyone likes you, or who is your coach.

All that matters is where the ball goes. This is the best part of golf for me.

I love that if you work hard, you get rewarded for that. It doesn't matter what anyone thinks.

I have been working hard on my golf game and practicing. This has led me to one little problem, MY TAN!

That tan I so wanted! Well, it is unfortunately not the kind of tan you want when you go to the pool.

We went to the Palm Woods CC pool today.

My feet were white, my left hand was white from wearing a glove, you could see a "v" around my neck, and I had lines across the top of my arms from my shirt.

Oh, and my legs, they had a mark across the top where my skirt stopped.

Golfers Tan

So yes, I have a tan, but it is a GOLFER'S TAN. I guess it is better than NO TAN AT ALL! ☺

April 24

Today my mom told me there is going to be a talent show at church. She asked me if I want to enter with my new bunny Putt, she thinks it would be cute.

I am so excited!!

I would love to show off my bunny Putt, but I need to teach him some tricks.

I RACK my brain and decide that maybe my bunny could knock stuff down if I put it in front of him.

I start putting things in front of him and trying to get him to run into it.

This may not be a bad idea...he seems to be doing okay at it.

When I put some pencils down for him to try to hop over...he picks one up and throws it with his mouth.

I am dying laughing, but then I start to think.

HMMMMMMM.

I could teach my bunny to knock down some upside down tees, push golf balls with his nose into a cup, and pick up a pencil and hand it to me so I can write his score.

I think this will work!

I am going to spend the next few days going over and over this routine. I sure hope it works.

I am going to put Putt in intensive bunny training!

After 30 minutes of training, Putt seems to be worn out and needs to take a break, so we decided to go to the range and practice for a bit.

I ran into Mackenzie and her mom, as I was going to the driving range to practice today.

I wanted to be nice so I said, "Hey Mackenzie, I really like your shirt."

She said, "Thanks, I really like yours too."

We both like pink.

I really do think she is nice and we could be friends.

I think her mom is crazy but I have 5 years of experience in dealing with crazy ice moms. I think a crazy golf mom should be a breeze.

As I am getting warmed up on the range, I am feeling so frustrated! I don't know what has been going on, but for some reason I have NOT been hitting the ball as well as I was.

My coach has me changing my swing path.

She says that it is hard to fix but once I fix this, I will be a lot more consistent.

In the meantime, I am NOT hitting the

ball well, and it is not much fun!

I still love golf, but the last couple times I hit golf balls I have been very discouraged by this process of changing my swing path. ☹

To make matters worse, the last time I went to the driving range this older gentleman would NOT STOP trying to help me.

I know he was trying to be nice but I really just wanted him to leave me alone.

I wanted to tell him, *I pay a coach to give me advice, and that is who I am going*

to listen to.

But I didn't - I just smiled, nodded, and said "Okay, thanks."

As I am hitting golf balls trying to work out my slump, I look over and OMG, Tyler is setting up next to me to hit balls.

He, of course, looks CUTE as ever!

He can tell I am frustrated, and he walks over and tells me I have a nice swing.

I am thinking in my head, *It feels like an awful swing to me right now.*

I know he is trying to be nice and I am sure he probably has been here himself. I say, "Thanks," smile and tell him he has an amazing swing!

He then asks me if I am going to play any holes today after I warm up.

In my head, I am dying!

I want to say YES, YES, YES, but I know I am in a slump and am too embarrassed to play with him right now.

I told him I can't today because I am trying to train my bunny for a talent show and I am really struggling with getting him to cooperate.

He smiles at me and says, "Well good luck with that!"

He then asks, "Where is the talent show going to be held and maybe I can come?"

I tell him it is at our church and where our church is located and that it is only 5 days away.

He then says, "I will ask my mom if I can come."

I am freaking out and wanting to scream at the same time!!

As if my bunny performing is not enough pressure, now my crush, Tyler wants to come and watch.

We both continue hitting balls and then he says he is going to go play a few holes and maybe we can play together sometime soon.

I told him, "Of course, I would love that!!!!"

Honestly, I would love to play with him today except for this stupid slump!!!

As I start to hit balls again, ANOTHER older man wants to give me some pointers.

I know if I was hitting the ball really well

this wouldn't keep happening, but honestly I need to just fix this by hitting balls on my own.

I WILL figure this out!

I already have too much going through my head. The last thing I need is someone, who is NOT a professional, talking to me about what they think will help me.

I try to smile and be nice AGAIN, but it doesn't work.

Then I remembered, at my last golf lesson I told my coach about people trying to help me on the range.

She said I should stop what I am doing, turn and face them, let it go in one ear and out the other, and then return to what I was doing.

Filtering!

She says this is called filtering, and by stopping and looking at them it also lets them know they are keeping me from practicing.

The next person that tried to help me I decided to give it a try and what do you know, it worked!

I didn't have to be rude, but he stopped when he realized I had to stop what I was working on.

My coach helps me with my golf, but she is also kind of like my golf counselor, too!

I am a little worried about my slump because tomorrow is the day my mom scheduled us to play golf with Mackenzie and her mom.

I hope I hit the ball better than when I played with them last.

My dad told me one day I will go hit balls, and it will all just click.

I NEED THAT DAY TO BE TOMORROW!

I want them to see I have been working hard and have gotten better since we played in that tournament together, not worse. UGH!!!

April 25

Today is the day we are playing with Mackenzie and her crazy mom.

We decided to ride in a cart because it will speed things up.

I wish Mackenzie and I could drive in our own cart, but the rule is you must be 16 and have a driver's license. ☹

Sometimes, when no one is out on the course, my parents will let me and my brother drive the cart, and it is SO MUCH FUN!

But we will each have to ride with our moms today.

I was kind of excited to play with Mackenzie's mom because she is supposed to be really good. She is always putting the pressure on Mackenzie, so I wanted to see just how good she is!

Mackenzie and I teed off first.

On the first hole, we all four hit our tee shots well, and everyone was in the fairway.

I was so excited and hoping my slump was OVER!

My second shot didn't go so well for my mom or myself, but Mackenzie and her mom were both on the green.

They both 2 putted for a par, and then Mackenzie's mom began high fiving and celebrating their victory over beating us on the first hole. Wait...WHAT??

Par	4	
Name		
Maureen	4	
Mackenzie	4	
Chloe	6	
Claire	5	

I didn't realize we were competing against each other.

I think Mackenzie was a little embarrassed by her mom's behavior, but she wouldn't dare NOT go along with her CRAZY mom.

I felt like telling Maureen, Mackenzie's mom, "YOU WIN!" That we can resolve this now so we can enjoy the rest of the round.

They WILL beat us! I have been playing for 4 months, and Mackenzie has been playing for 9 years.

Her mom played college golf. My mom hadn't played since she had kids, which was 12 years ago!

We thought we were playing a friendly "who really cares about the formal rules" round, but boy were we in for a rude awakening!

On the next hole I was getting ready to tee off, when Mackenzie's mom jumped on the tee box and let me know that they got to tee off first because they had honors.

I wasn't trying to jump ahead. It is just that when my family plays for fun, we play "ready golf" **which means that whoever is ready goes**.

So I walked off the tee box with my golf ball in my hand, and let Mackenzie go first.

AGAIN...

I didn't know we signed up to "compete" against them!

I suddenly realized that this is not the fun outing I was hoping for.

They beat us on the 2nd hole, and Mackenzie even got a birdie.

She is playing really well.

I think she is better than the last time I played with her, which was at my first junior tournament.

Par	4	4
Name		
Maureen	4	4
Mackenzie	4	③
Chloe	6	5
Claire	5	5

When you get a birdie during the round, you circle the birdies on your scorecard.

I was happy for her and told her, "Good birdie."

She just smiled, nodded, acting cool (in front of her mom) and said, "Oh thanks."

I wonder if she is acting this way because it is what her mom expects.

I heard her tell her mom. "I am one under par now. I sure wish Grandpa was here to see how well I am playing."

By now I AM NOT feeling this whole thing.

But, off to the 3rd tee box we went. I hit a horrible shot, AGAIN!

I obviously HAVE NOT pulled out of my slump!!

I was hoping I would have come out of it by today and be hitting the ball great.

I have no idea when the slump is going to go away.

Today would be a good time for it to happen!

Even though I am in my slump, I do know that I must stay focused and concentrate.

When I stopped concentrating, because I got upset, I totally lost what little golf swing I had left.

I only hit the ball about 3 feet off the tee box.

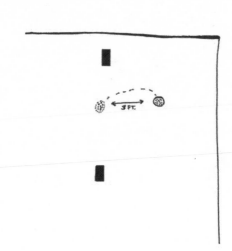

If it were just my mom and I she would have told me to hit another ball.

I mean, I am still learning.

But with these two and how serious the circumstances are, I didn't dare hit a second ball.

I walked up to my second shot and did my pre shot routine, but unfortunately, I duffed it again, and it went toward the woods and into the deep rough.

Mrs. Maureen and Mackenzie both hit their balls in the fairway and were looking back at my mom and me like we were holding them up.

This is such an awful feeling!!!!

I was ready to cry!

I went to my ball in the deep rough.

I don't have much experience in the deep

rough. I did what I would do if I were in the fairway.

I got out my 3-wood because it is the longest club I have, and I was a long way from the hole.

Well, I only hit it about 15 yards and I AM STILL IN THE ROUGH!

I was so DONE!!!!!

I wanted to pick my ball up and just go home!

My mom suggested I take an iron and punch the ball out into the fairway to get the ball back in play.

I decided to hit my favorite iron, my 7-iron.

Thankfully, I hit my ball out of the rough.

I guess the lesson I learned from this is that when you are in the deep rough you have to change your next shot.

Sometimes it is best to **hit a punch shot out of the rough, and get the ball in a good place for the next shot.**

But, really at this point, I was NOT having much fun!

My mom was hitting the ball okay, but I know she felt bad for me.

The only thing I could do was count down how many holes we had left to play.

I was hoping we were only playing 9 holes, because I couldn't take playing all 18 under these conditions!

Just as I was to my breaking point, I decided to walk up to my next shot, calm down, and pull myself together.

And that is just what I did!

My golf coach tells me I hit the ball best when I relax and don't try so hard.

I was at my wit's end, and this was my plan - to relax, not try so hard, and try to have fun.

I walked up to the ball, took a deep

breath, and hit the ball way down the fairway.

One thing I have learned about golf is nothing feels better than hitting the ball well and nothing feels worse than hitting the ball poorly!

I was experiencing both of those feelings on this one hole!

However, I did seem to be back on track - somewhat.

We got up to the green and guess what we heard.

You got it, more celebrating. Mackenzie's mom was saying that they were EVEN PAR through 3 holes and killing it.

Blah! Blah! Blah!

ANNOYED

Even though I had a terrible hole, I tried to smile and tell Mackenzie and her mom, "Great Job!" But under my breath I was thinking, *OMG you 2 are crazy!*

I don't think Mackenzie is crazy.

She seems like she is feeling bad, but doesn't want her crazy mom scolding her, so she is just going along.

I have seen up close how crazy her mom can be, and I don't blame her for just going along.

I think we could be good friends, in spite of her mom, but it will have to be at the golf course, WITHOUT HER MOM!

New hole, new start, that was going to be my motto for the 4th hole.

When we get over to the next tee box, the mother, Maureen, puts her hand on my shoulder and says to me, "Honey, would you like to hit from the children's tees?"

The children's tees are fake tee boxes in the middle of the fairway.

I was so MAD that she would say this!

I thought she was going to be encouraging to me – you know, girl to girl.

This was the furthest thing from it.

What her comment did do, was get me FIRED UP!

I stood on that tee box, from the regular ladies tees and smashed the ball! It felt great!

I wanted to say to her, *What was that you said again?*

It was no big surprise that they "beat us" on the 4th hole. I mean, we haven't won a hole yet, but honestly, we didn't care!

There was a bathroom on the way from the 4th green to the 5th tee.

We stopped to use the restroom and Mackenzie's mom says, "Um, I was just thinking, to make things fair we would play low ball."

Low ball is when you count the score of the person from a team who had the lowest score on the hole.

Well, I may only be 12, but I can tell you one thing that is pretty easy to figure out....

WE WON'T BE USING MY SCORES!

Double Annoyed!!

My mother steps in and says, "Well, that is not going to help us at all. You can play 'lowball' between the two of you."

I just don't get it! Don't they know we:

> 1. Are not good enough to compete with them.

> 2. Are choosing NOT to compete against them.

My mom and I continued to the 5th tee box.

By this time the whole situation has

become comical!

My mom and I decided we would just do our own thing, and let them do their own thing.

I walk up to the 5th tee, and hit the ball on the sweet spot of my club.

When you hit the sweet spot of your club, you can REALLY hit the ball far.

That is just what I did.

I hit the ball so far that I outdrove my mom and both Mackenzie and her mom, the college player.

Funny thing though, even when I felt like crying on the 3rd hole, I told them, "Good shot, great job, etc."

I smashed the ball down the middle of the fairway, outdriving everyone, and not one comment from either Mackenzie or her mom.

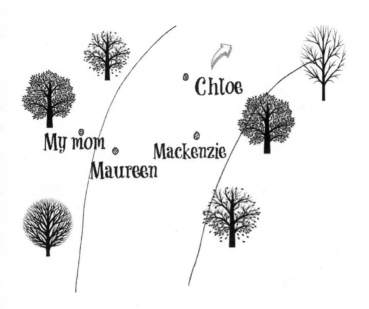

My mom was thrilled for me, and she told me what a great shot I had hit. It really felt good!

We played holes #6,7.

When driving up to number 8 my mom and I could not be happier!

We were laughing and celebrating that this whole thing was almost over.

I knew that my mom would handle not

playing more than nine holes because we were DONE!

I asked my mom, "What are you going to do if they tell us to keep playing after the 9th hole?"

She replied, "We are NOT playing," as she was laughing.

But that told me with certainty not to worry, that we WERE DONE after 9!

Hallelujah!

I was so happy to be on the 9th tee box.

This not-so-fun social was almost over, but not without one more dig!

We all hit our tee shots on number 9, which is a par 3.

My mom and Mackenzie's mom were on the green, and Mackenzie and myself were in the sand.

Mackenzie was closer to the green so I was to hit first. My dad told me a couple of **basic tips for hitting out of the sand. One was to aim a little left of the flag when you get your feet set, and two was to hit about 1 inch behind the ball to allow the sand to move the ball out of the trap.**

I focused on those 2 things, and surprisingly I hit it out and 6 inches from the hole. I was so excited! I have a tap in to par the hole!

Mackenzie hit her sand shot next and it went 15 feet past the cup.

I one-putted and ended the round on a happy "Par," which I hadn't had for the day.

Mackenzie got a bogey on the hole.

It was just killing her mom that on the

last hole I beat her score. She says to my mom, "Did you see Mackenzie hit the fried egg out of the sand trap?"

My mom turned and looked at her and said, "A fried egg? What are you talking about?"

Her mom goes on to explain that **when a ball is buried under the sand to where all you can see is the top half of the ball, they call this a fried egg.**

She said, "They are very hard to hit and Mackenzie just hit it out like a pro!"

I looked at my mom and she looked at me. We shrugged our shoulders, smiled, and walked toward our golf cart.

I don't care what she wants to call Mackenzie's golf shots. I am only concerned about one thing...BEING DONE!!

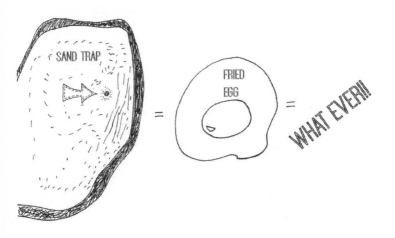

I was looking forward to a relaxing round with friendly people, but this felt like anything but that.

I felt like I WAS the fried egg, and I wanted out of the hot skillet!

Today I decided that the best way to end my slump was to go and hit tons of balls at the driving range. Maybe this way the slump will leave sooner rather than later.

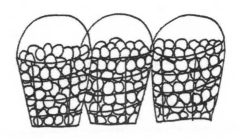

After hitting balls for a while at the range my mom, my brother, and I decided we would play a few holes.

Sometimes, it is so hot on the driving range that we don't hit balls very long.

We go play holes because driving the cart gives us a breeze.

Of course Caleb and I never agree. I usually want to play the front 9, because that is what we play for tournaments.

And Caleb always wants to play the back 9. Why, I do not know!

As we are driving over to the front 9 to see if we can play, we run into Maureen and Mackenzie Jones.

We are nice and exchange pleasantries.

After playing with them yesterday, there is NO WAY I am going to play with them today!

We wait to see if they are going to play, because if they are, I am not teeing off right now!

I love how peaceful golf is, and I am quickly becoming picky about who I am willing to play with.

I wouldn't mind playing with Mackenzie, but I will never play with her mom again!

I must keep golf relaxing, and she is NOT relaxing.

We see them walking over to the driving range.

It looks like we are in the clear to tee off.

We go to the 1st tee. We all hit our drives, our second shots, and as we are getting onto the 1st green, we see a woman and her daughter behind us.

I look back, and the woman has on an orange shirt with dots (the same as Mrs. Maureen) – I am thinking, *are you kidding me!*

We are a 3 some and they are a 2 some.

I am sure they are going to try to catch up to us so they can join us.

3 ⚬ 2 = **NOt HAppening**

That is the last thing I want!

It will be stressful and no fun!

All the mom wants to do, is compare me to Mackenzie, and I already know that Mackenzie is better than I am right now, and will beat me.

She just did it yesterday!

I am here to have a fun, relaxing afternoon. She and her mom will be anything but that!

We quickly go to the 2nd tee. We try to

hit our tee shots and quickly go to our second shots, but this is not going to work.

We are 3 people, they are 2 people, plus they are better golfers than we are. They are going to catch us!

We all hit our second shots and none of us hit them very well. We were feeling so rushed!!

My mom says, "Pick up your golf balls. We are going to cut through and jump on the back 9 holes."

Chloe   Caleb

As we pick up our golf balls, we turn and see that they are teeing off on the 2nd tee box.

We watch their tee shots, and honestly, Mackenzie's shot looked really good.

Caleb says, "Mackenzie looks like she has gotten even better."

At that moment, we tore out of there and head to the back 9.

Usually, late in the day, it is not a problem to jump to the back 9.

Well, wouldn't it be our luck...the back 9 was loaded up. We were not going to get out for a while.

We need a new plan. My mom says, "We are driving up and starting the front 9 over."

As we are driving up to the front 9 we pass the driving range and see Mrs. Maureen (in her orange shirt with dots) and Mackenzie are still on the driving range hitting balls.

Orange shirt big dots! OOPS

I tell my mom, "OMG!!!! That was not the Jones behind us!"

So my mom in a state of panic spins the cart around to try to reclaim our spot on the front nine at the 3rd hole. She turns the cart so sharply that the cart turns on its side on 2 wheels.

My brother screams at my mom, "MOM

WHAT ARE YOU DOING???"

I was holding on for dear life.

By the time we returned to the 3rd tee box, WE WERE FRAZZLED!!!

I told my mom, "This is crazy! The people were NOT the Jones!"

It was an easy mistake because both adults had the same colored shirt with slightly different dots.

I was so flustered after all that craziness it was hard to settle down to play golf.

I didn't hit the ball very well and I told my mom it was her fault because of how frazzled I was!

My mom said, "Well, this is good practice for handling stressful situations."

I think it is good practice for handling a crazy mom, and I don't know how that is going to help my golf game.

We finally got settled down enough to collect our thoughts and my brother says, "MOM, I think you did a doughnut on the grass, and it might have torn up the grass a bit."

My mom said that she will drive back when there aren't so many people and we will look and see. There is no way she is going up there right now after the embarrassing ruckus we just created.

She said if the grass is torn up, she will go in the golf pro shop and offer to pay for repairs.

<u>One thing that is a must in golf is taking care of the golf course. You are supposed to be cautious and repair any damage you do</u>.

Thankfully when we went back up to see if there was any damage, there wasn't.

I am so glad because I have had enough drama for one day!

I am STILL WAITING FOR THE SLUMP TO GO AWAY!

I am so discouraged!

I know I have gone through similar times in figure skating.

For example, it took me one whole year to learn how to do an Axel jump. An Axel jump is where you spin around in the air 1 1/2 times.

If I can stick with that for a year, I know I will come out of this golf slump in a shorter time than that.

Skating has taught me some good mental skills that help me in golf.

I wouldn't mind skating again, but just for fun. I don't like the competitive arena of skating.

I still haven't said anything to my mom about not wanting to return to figure skating.

Sometimes I can tell she wants to say something to me, but she doesn't. It is getting tense and weird...I have to figure out how to have this talk.

I don't know how much more weird tension I can take!

Today I am not feeling well at all!!

I have a sinus infection that I have had for a few days. I really don't feel like playing golf today.

It is a chance to play on one of the most expensive golf courses in our city. And, it's the last PGA Junior league match of the season. I decide to go to the match today.

We get to the course, and I go to the driving range to warm up. Every shot I hit I am hooking the ball.

A hook is when you hit the ball and it curves severely to the left.

Hook

My dad is trying to help me, but honestly nothing he says is really HELPING AT ALL.

As a matter of fact, he is creating some stress for me!!

We get to the first tee box. My partner for today is Joey. We are paired with 3 little 8 year olds (only 2 play at a time, they will rotate who plays which holes).

They are all in matching outfits, matching bags, and even matching clubs, and they are all equally annoying!!!

I am hoping at this point that I can pull myself together and hit a good shot off the first tee.

I am just SO TIRED OF NOT HITTING THE BALL WELL!!!!!

I am channeling all my best thoughts!!

I get up and hit my tee shot, and you guessed it...I hooked it. It was an awful shot.

I am hoping that my partner can save us and hit a good shot.

It turns out to be wishful thinking, because he also hits a bad shot. ☹

The little babies get up and hit their shots.

It doesn't take much to out drive us, and when they do, they are celebrating, high fiving, and well, it's annoying.

I was determined to dig deep and try hard to hit good shots. Honestly, that made me mad to see them do that.

I wanted to put them in their place.

I will save the painful details of the first 3 holes but Joey and I played awful!!

It seemed like the harder we tried the worse we hit the ball.

It was so frustrating!!!

AND...the brats captured the first flag.

I could NOT believe it!

I was so mad! I was going to try even harder to hit the ball well.

For the next set of 3 holes, my partner Joey, found his swing. He came alive!

He was killing the ball, and he hit some amazing shots!

Me...I had a few good shots here and there, but honestly I was frustrated! I just wanted to go HOME!!!

I then decided I would try to make a difference on the putting green, and see if I could help out that way.

I did make some good putts, so I felt a little better about finding some way to help out. We ended up capturing the 2nd flag and HOLY MOLY, what a brat baby show!!!

Captured

When we captured the 2nd flag, they were so MAD!

They were throwing their clubs and wouldn't walk to the next hole. Their moms had to yell at them until they finally dragged up to the next hole.

As much as they celebrated at the beginning...well, they threw an equally attention-getting tantrum.

We were getting ready to start the last set of 3 holes. We have each captured one flag.

I get up to the tee, and I really hit a

great drive for me.

I had my fingers crossed that I was pulling out of my slump for the last 3 holes. NOT SO LUCKY!

My next shot was back to the horrible golf I had been playing.

I decided to take the good shots when I could and continue to make a difference in putting!

We were all tied up as we came down to the last hole.

I was REALLY NOT wanting these brats to beat us!

I wanted to give it everything I had, but honestly, I was so confused, because it seemed like when I tried really hard, it went so badly!

When I didn't try at all...I hit a good shot. It was so confusing!

On the 9th and final hole, we were both on the green in 3 shots, and we both had putts that were about 15 feet away from the cup.

It would all come down to the one who could make a putt.

The Brats were slightly further away so they went first. They made good putts but missed.

This was a chance for Joey and I to concentrate and win.

Joey went first. He hit the ball just a little to the right of the cup. I placed my ball on the green and looked at the hole from all angles.

It did help to see the break and speed of the greens from Joey's putt, but I was feeling pressure.

It was so quiet, you could hear a pin drop!

I stood over the ball with confidence and

made my putting stroke. It felt like the ball was rolling in slow motion.

The ball rolled right up to the cup and dropped in the hole.

We won the match! I was so excited!

I wasn't striking the ball well, but found a way to contribute, and help us win the match.

It showed me how important good putting really is!

However, the most difficult lesson I learned today was that the harder I try, the worse I play.

That seems so backward for me, because the last thing I want to do is not try and not give it my all.

I really need to figure out how this whole trying harder/doing worse thing works.

I just don't get it!

I talked to my dad (my expert at golf) when I got home, and told him I had 2 questions and I needed his help!

1. What can I do to settle down before the first hole of my golf match? It takes me 3 holes to relax and feel comfortable.

2. Why does it seem as though the harder I try the worse I play?

For the first question, he said when I am

warming up on the driving range, I needed to pretend I am actually playing the first few holes. This will help me relax and calm myself.

He said I needed to pull out my driver and see how far it goes. Then, select my next club and visualize myself playing an actual hole.

He says this should help me settle down. That way when I step on the first tee box, it should feel like my 4th or 5th hole of the match.

I am going to try this. It does seem like it should help!

For the trying harder problem, he said golf is about learning to relax. The more tightly you hold the club, the worse things go on the course. Check my grip and make sure I am not squeezing the club.

That was great advice!

My dad always knows how to help me in golf.

Well, I have some advice I would like to give the BRAT BABIES.

"When you lose, say very little, and when you win say even less!" They need to learn this, because all the celebrating they did over capturing the first flag was not necessary! If they are good, we will know! They don't need to tell us!

Today is the Bunny Talent Show at church.

I was so nervous! I wondered if my bunny was going to perform his tricks.

We arrive at church, and as we were getting ready, everyone wanted to hold my bunny.

I didn't want Putt's nerves to get shot by all the little kids passing him around. I told everyone that after the show, I would let them have a turn to pet him.

Earlier, I had asked my brother Caleb to be my assistant.

His jobs were to help me get the tees set up for Putt to knock down, get the little mini golf course set up with a hole for Putt to push the ball in, and stand to the side if I needed anything else.

Honestly, it made me feel a little better not being on the stage by myself. I liked having him there.

They called my name and we walked onto the stage.

We got everything set up, and it was time to start.

My mom was narrating over a speaker and she started the story.

She said, "Hi. My name is Putt, and I like to play golf. Each day as I head to the tee box I first pick which color tee I want to use. Blue is my favorite color so I always pick the blue tee."

I am really hoping Putt picks the right color tee! As he inches his nose forward he knocks down the blue tee. YAY!

I let out a huge sigh of relief and I smile and wave to the audience.

I then pick Putt up and place him on the artificial green with the ball and cup as my mom continues.

"After I tee off, I go to the fairway and hit my next shot onto the green. I then head to the green and I am ready to putt. I am really good at one putting."

I place the ball in front of him and Putt then takes a hop forward, pushes the ball with his nose and it goes in the cup.

YAY PUTT!

I am so happy and relieved.

Everyone clapped as he hit the ball in the cup.

We are almost done, and he is performing wonderfully!!!

My mom continues her narration, "After Putt makes his birdie putt, we need to record your score Putt."

I pick Putt up and place him behind the pencil on the table. At this time Putt picks up the pencil with his teeth, tosses it in my direction, and I catch the pencil.

Good Job!

I do a curtsy bow. I pick Putt up and hold him high in the air.

The crowd cheers and claps. As I look around the audience, I see Tyler. He is clapping, cheering, and then I see him wink at me. Caleb and I walk around to the front of the stage and grab hands. We take another bow and walk off the stage.

It felt so amazing, and I am so proud of Putt for his perfect performance!

Caleb and I head to sit in the audience.

I find Tyler and we sit beside him. I hand Putt to him and introduce him to my bunny.

He said he loves animals and pets Putt on the head, and continues to hold him.

I love my little bunny, and I am so proud of him!

Once the show was over, they were ready to announce the winner of the show.

I really felt like Putt had a chance to win, but I didn't want to get my hopes up because then I would be disappointed, if he didn't win.

Everyone did so well! It could really go to anyone.

I am jostling my knee up and down as we are waiting. I can hardly take it.

They announce the 3rd place winner, and it was a couple that sang a country song together.

They were actually really good.

Then the announcer says that there is only 1 vote separating 1st and 2nd place. I am feeling so nervous!

I wish they would just say it - it feels like they are going so slowly!

They announce that 2nd place was a little 4 year-old-girl that played her guitar and sang a sweet song.

I am so nervous!

I am thinking that maybe they were

looking for singers because 2nd and 3rd place both went to singers.

OMG!!!!

Say it already! Who is 1st place?

They then announce that 1st place was a routine that they had never seen before.

It was very entertaining and unique.

Tyler looks at me and says, "Relax you got this!"

They announce that 1st place goes to PUTT, THE BUNNY!!!!!

Tyler hands Putt back to me. Everyone is clapping! Caleb and I go running up to the stage with Putt. They hand us a trophy for 1st place, and I cannot believe my bunny has won a trophy.

Yay Putt!!!

I am so happy and proud of my bunny!
Caleb and I cannot stop smiling!!

I love my bunny Putt, and I am so glad
the Easter Bunny brought me such a
sweet and talented bunny!

April 30

So many amazing things have happened in the past month.

It has been the best month of my life!

I have learned to play golf, made some GFF's, met a cute boy, and got a bunny!

I just have one thing I need to do...I need to have a talk with my mom about figure skating.

I don't miss it, and I don't want to go back to spending 6 days a week in a rink for hours a day...I CAN NOT DO IT!!

It is so stressful, and I think it is crazy for my mom to pay so much money for me to be stressed out!

I have not had one moment of real stress from golf, even in my slump!

It is so fun and something I can't wait to do.

 Golf

My mom is standing at the sink doing dishes. I walk in the kitchen and tell her that I need to talk to her.

She says, "Sure, honey, let me dry my hands and I will be right there."

I go in the living room and I am sitting on the couch waiting for her to come in.

She walks in, sits down, and I say to her,

"Mom I don't know where to start. Since I hurt my knee, and I haven't been skating, I have really enjoyed NOT going to the rink and NOT dealing with the crazy schedule. I LOVE feeling so much less stressed! I also really love playing golf! I never thought golf would be so much fun, but I love it! The people are so nice and everything about it is fun! I also like being able to play with the whole family!"

My mom gives me a smile and tilts her head to the side and runs her hand down the side of my hair. She pulls me to her chest and gives me a hug and says, "Honey, I have been watching you and I already knew you were loving golf. A year ago your Aunt Jana had a talk with me and told me she thought you were skating for me. Well, I have been watching you, and I knew she was right and that you were not having much fun doing it anymore. I am so glad you have found what you love."

I asked my mom, "But what about my skating outfits for this upcoming year? You have already bought them, and my new skates, and all the money you have spent."

My mom replied, "Don't worry about that!" With a big smile on her face, she said, "Think of all the money we will save by you not skating," as she giggled.

She said, "I love playing golf, and we can all go out and play together. It will be good exercise for me to get back to playing. I am thrilled by your decision, but more importantly, I am proud of you for coming to me and telling me your true feelings. I have been waiting for when you were going to tell me what was going on in that sweet little head of yours."

There it is. My mom is happy for me! I am
so relieved, and I am looking forward to
all the golf fun that is in my future!

About the Author:

Gwen Elizabeth Foddrell is from Richmond,
Virginia. She is a true animal lover,
especially her bunny, Toby. She loves to
organize, decorate, and do-it-yourself
projects. She loves all things girl, like nail
polish, heels, and jewelry. She loves her
newly found sport of golf and hanging
with her family and friends...and of
course, she is always up for girl talk!

I want to thank my Papa for inspiring me to write furiously, without caution. I want to thank my Brother for giving me good material and being my true friend. And finally, I want to thank my Mom and Dad for being an amazing support team, and making my dreams come true! I LOVE YOU ALL!

Angry

Feeling it

Maybe

Done!

Confused

Doggie

Uncertain

Worried

Mad

Made in the USA
Middletown, DE
17 May 2015